PRAIS

"THE DEVOURER FROM BEYOND"

"RK Jack's *The Devourer From Beyond* turns the knob up to eleven then breaks it off. Nonstop action, chills, and a terrific storyline that sets a pace faster than *Raiders of the Lost Ark* and continues to deliver."
—Mark Everett Stone, author of *Things to Do in Denver When You're Un-Dead*

"In *The Devourer From Beyond*, RK Jack combines various genres to create a gripping page-turner. The author adeptly conveys the law enforcement representatives' way of thinking and their perception of hazardous circumstances, increasing the psychological and emotional depth of the narration. An enthralling twist promises more breathtaking discoveries, and the conclusion does not disappoint."
—*Readers' Favorite* 5-Star Review by Nino Lobiladze

ARGENT

RK JACK

CONTENTS

PART I
GREENLOVE VILLAGE

Chapter 1   3
Chapter 2   17

PART II
HALLOWDALE FOREST

Chapter 3   41
Chapter 4   61

PART III
THE TOMB

Chapter 5   83
Chapter 6   99

PART IV
EPILOGUE

Chapter 7   113

Acknowledgments   119
About the Author   121
Connect with the Author   123

ARGENT

Published by Horizon View Press LLC

Denver, CO

Copyright © 2025 by Russell Jack (RK Jack). All rights reserved.

This book is a work of fiction. All names, characters, and events that occur are fictitious. Thus, any relationship to any person, living or dead, or actual events is coincidental.

No part of this book may be reproduced in any form or by any mechanical means, including information storage and retrieval systems, without permission in writing from the publisher/author, except by a reviewer who may quote passages in a review. For information on permissions or to contact the author, visit rkjackauthor.com.

All images, logos, quotes, and trademarks included in this book are subject to use according to trademark and copywriting laws of the United States of America.

ISBN: 979-8-9900568-3-1 Paperback

ISBN: 979-8-9900568-5-5 Hardcover

FIC009120   **FICTION** / Fantasy / Dragons & Mythical Creatures

Cover design and copyright owned by Russell Jack (RK Jack).

All rights reserved by Russell Jack (RK Jack) and Horizon View Press LLC.

To my mother—
Who is also a creature of good.

PART I

GREENLOVE VILLAGE

CHAPTER 1

DARROW

Greenlove Village is the only home I've ever known. No one knows precisely when it was founded, as it gradually evolved from an outpost to a hamlet and then to a village over a century or two. It has only a few thousand inhabitants but is situated near one of the common trade routes in a valley next to the Hallowdale Forest. Technically, it is a town, and that is what most of us call it.

When I am not in school, I work for Micah, the village blacksmith. It has its perks, as I get to play with real swords and axes and make them! When I am older, I want to do the same as Micah. As the village only needed one blacksmith, however, I would have to make my way to another village or town, maybe even a city.

But not today.

Today, I asked Grace to join me for an adventure, and I had a destination in mind—one sure to surprise her. We liked calling them that, but it was really just us taking turns surprising each other with where we would walk next.

Sometimes, we just hunted with bows, with the bonus of sometimes bringing back fresh game to give to Gretchen, Grace's mom. Other times, we would get our shinais, which are made with long, thin wooden strips banded together to make practice swords. Unlike the heavier bokkens, which were one solid piece of heavy wood, we could hit each other with the shinai without injury.

We were preparing for the great battles we would never have...

I had to admit that Grace had the upper hand; she won more of our "fights" than she lost, but I was growing and was already nearly equal in height and strength to her. In a couple more years, I will be bigger and stronger.

Today, we were simply walking. However, we always carried our real bows and swords as part of our feeling of being "on an adventure."

The wind was whispering through the pines and made a relaxing sound as I walked with my best friend, Grace. We had snuck off to have a picnic on the forest's edge just outside the village.

Graciela, or just Grace to her friends, is a wonderful young woman, and I genuinely enjoy spending time with her. She had grown to a tall woman of 17 hands of height and weighed a fit and lean 12 stone. She had beautiful, long, wavy red hair and a pretty, freckled face from being in the sun. With deep green eyes and a genuinely happy smile, she was everything I dreamed of in a woman.

We grew up as friends since we were small children, and always acted like the best of friends we were. Over the last couple of years, though, I have started to develop feelings for her, but I don't think she knows or would ever reciprocate them. She sees me as the younger brother she never had. We only have a four-year age difference, but when you're eighteen, I understand that fourteen is still relatively young.

I sighed.

"Everything OK there, little slug?"

She has called me "little slug" for as long as I can remember. It seems I hardly ever went by Darrow in her presence, which was fine by me—I liked her pet name for me.

"Yeah, just thinking," I replied.

"About…?" she asked.

"Oh, just about where our lives will go soon. I like you, and I know it won't be long before you leave the village."

Part of me hoped she would figure out that she had grown into a beautiful young woman and that I wanted to be more than just a friend to her. The other part hoped she didn't—so it would not hurt our friendship. If she noticed, she did a good job pretending she didn't.

"Oh, Darrow, you are such a softie!" she punched my arm playfully.

I laughed, and we continued walking until we came to a stop by the edge of Hallowdale Forest.

"Here's the spot. Care for a bite before our great journey?" I asked.

"Please," she replied, with that beautiful smile of hers.

Taking a large, thin blanket from my backpack, we spread it out and sat down. After unpacking, we were settled. We began to eat, and the food from the Lemur was excellent. She had brought along a bottle of mead, as well as sausages, cheeses, and bread—perks of her job. The pub where Grace worked as a barmaid was named "The One-Eyed Lemur," but everyone in the village simply referred to it as "the Lemur."

Satiated, we lay back to stare into the beautiful blue sky. Fluffy clouds floated by, and I enjoyed the scents. I could smell the pine and a whiff of lavender on the wind. The lavender was from her perfume, which caused me to have to tamp my arousal.

I wish I did not love her.

Of course, she did not know, and I would never tell her; some things are just never to be revealed.

We decided to take a kip…

The wind woke us. It was only midday, and she would not have to go back to work until tonight, so we still had plenty of time.

"Want to go for a walk?" I asked.

"Sure, where to this time?" she responded with another beautiful smile.

"It is a surprise," I replied.

"Alright, lead the way, slug."

I did. After putting everything back into my pack, it was time for adventure!

Striding with purpose, we headed through the Hallowdale Forest until we got to a clearing. The wind was now a steady, almost mournful sound, along with the crunching of the thin layer of snow underfoot. The hint of the winter to come hung heavy in the air, as it had recently snowed, but I knew we had a month or so of fall before the winter truly began...

"Slug, what are you doing?" she asked. This time, with a seriousness that let me know I was doing something I shouldn't.

"Don't you want to know what is inside?"

We were standing near the edge of Amorak Cemetery.

"Nope. I know exactly where *my* dead kin are, and they aren't going anywhere near here. Just like we shouldn't," she scolded.

She had buried her father at the village's new graveyard, Greenlove Cemetery, only four years ago. He had died of the coughing-lung disease. None of us knew what it was, but others had died of the same illness over the years. It was nothing ominous, as it was still reasonably rare. His grave was far from this abandoned graveyard and in the opposite direction from the village.

The village elders had forbidden anyone to enter this graveyard after several people had disappeared there over the years. Each had headed out on their own, without telling anyone, only never to return.

Older adults are always so superstitious.

The people probably just wanted to leave the village without "upsetting" the people they left behind; at least, that is my thought on the matter.

"Grace, you and I both know it is superstition; there is no monster lurking in there. Those townspeople just left, and the elders don't want us townies to say the obvious. They didn't die here; they left from here to get out of Greenlove."

Part of me *was* a little scared, but I didn't want Grace to think I was chicken, so I purposely strode into the graveyard. I looked back at her from a gravestone. She just shrugged and followed me onto the hallowed but forbidden grounds.

"It is kinda neat just to be doing bad," she said with a smirk.

I winked at her, and she winked back.

If only I were older...

The graveyard was massive. Stretching out a quarter of a league across, it held a variety of tombstones, from simple stone markers flat to the ground to elaborate stone ones and every variation between. If I am being honest with myself, it was really a beautiful and peaceful place—an eternal home to thousands.

We walked until we got to the mausoleum at the cemetery's center.

The mausoleum was also large—a good thirty meters in diameter—and was said to hold catacombs below. The age-worn stone gargoyles atop the building eyed us malevolently. Even I was too scared to go in.

There was also a different smell here. Maybe it was the huckleberries or some of the other plants, but it was weird compared to what we were used to.

"Darrow, what is that?"

She was pointing at one of the graves near the mausoleum.

I looked where she was pointing and saw it—a glint of metal in the sun's midday glare.

We walked over, and I knelt. There was nothing else to see; it was just the tiniest smudge of a golden sheen on the ground. I started digging around it with my hands, unearthing something buried just below...

She gasped as I pulled it from the earth.

It was a crown!

As I buffed and cleaned the dirt from it, I was in awe as well.

"Oh, my Lord! What have we found?" she asked with worry.

It was a magnificent crown, made entirely from a single piece of the purest gold and encrusted with a king's fortune in precious gems as well.

My insides tightened in fear.

To most, it would be the find of a lifetime. However, for ordinary villagers, something of this value is the kind of thing that draws attention from the highest rulers in the land. The King and the Lords of the land would be coming if they found out we had this. Worse, they would ask us *where* we found it...

"Put it back, Darrow. Put it back and bury it!" she said.

"No way, it's ours! This will fetch enough for you never to have to work as a barmaid again. You and I could run away to wherever we wanted—"

Oh no!

I had blurted that out without even realizing what I said!

The look on her face told me she understood *exactly* what I meant.

"Oh, Darrow..." she said, touching my shoulder.

"You and I are never going to be more than friends. You are turning into a strapping young lad, but I don't want us to lose the friendship we already have."

I felt despair as I had never felt before—she had answered my unasked question, which I had kept secret for so long. There would be no romantic "we". Ever.

Looking at the priceless crown in my hand, I had an overwhelming urge—

I placed the crown on my head.

Suddenly, I felt powerful. In fact, I was too important to be ignored!

"How about now? Now that I am your king! Would you still turn down my hand and cast me aside?" I yelled.

She looked at me in abject terror.

"Darrow! This isn't like you! Take it off! Take it off!" she screamed.

"Never! This is mine! No one shall ever stand in my way; I am Vzerie; I am your king!"

My vision blurred, and I felt a horrible agony

wracking my body. My last moments alive were spent seeing the horrified look on my beloved's face...

* * *

GRACIELA

I KNEW I should not have let Darrow bring me here!
The elders' declaration that the graveyard was off-limits *was* silly. This was not our first foray into the cemetery; we had done it as young children. Even now, I can almost feel the lashings on my behind. My mother, Gretchen, usually the sweetest woman you would ever meet, tanned my hide fiercely that day. I promised her I would never return.

And I had now broken my promise.

I also knew Darrow was starting to have feelings for me as a woman. Hoping he would figure out I was not interested in him that way, I deliberately ignored his increasingly less-than-subtle advances. However, now I was in tears as I lost my only best friend to lunacy.

He had placed the crown on his head and immediately descended into a scorned rage. Darrow had changed completely when he put on that crown. He had never spoken to me or anyone else like that. This wasn't like him at all. His features were so dark with anger, I could see his visage as one of pure evil; it was terrifying.

Slowly, I moved my hand to my sword.

He saw this and, for the briefest of moments, Darrow was back.

"Oh, my sweet Grace, forgive me—" he said in sorrow. AHHH!

He screamed in incomprehensible pain and anguish.

Before me, his head and body started to melt and decay before my very eyes!

Skin and blood ran down off him in putrid sheets, rivulets of blood and skin sloughing off of bones. Organs fell with horrible plopping noises as he continued screaming in unimaginable pain. His body fell into a pile of itself and moldered into a horrible-smelling pile of rotted goo before my eyes.

Without consciously thinking, I grabbed the crown and ran.

The sky above began to darken, and I could see thunderclouds. Their arrival felt anything but natural; the speed and ferocity of the approaching storms were otherworldly. Behind me, I heard the crack of lightning.

As I ran for the edge of the graveyard, I tucked the crown into my bag. That is when I saw tombstones start falling over and hands digging out from their earthen graves...

I WAS TERRIFIED.

If I could only go back an hour and stop Darrow from walking in...

However, I *hadn't* stopped him.

In fact, my guilt was all-consuming: It was I who agreed to go in, who pointed out the glint in the soil, and who told him his love was unrequited at the worst possible time.

Now, it seems that I will be atoning for all my sins.

The hands pulled out things from the ground. Some were clearly zombies, and, worse, some were ghouls and skeletons—and all were going to kill any living human in their midst.

And I was the only human in their midst.

One had pulled itself free and was standing before me; it was a zombie.

Zombies are corpses that have been reanimated by powerful necromancy. They were mindless but had an insatiable appetite for human flesh. The one before me was horrifying; it was missing one hand and eye, and parts of its mottled skin were missing. Rotting intestines were dangling out, swinging about as it moved.

It would prevent my escape, so I swung my blade with practiced ease. Many a tree branch had fallen to my attacks over the years, and I had trained with wooden swords against Darrow, but I had never been in actual combat before.

It silently reached out to grab me in its deadly embrace, but my sword found its neck—

SWISH, SMACK—thump

The zombie's head fell to the earth as its headless

body joined it a moment later. Fear drove me into a sprint for the edge of the forest.

I almost made it.

Stopping suddenly and painfully, I screamed as a hand grabbed my ankle and refused to let go. I felt something make a painful "pop" in my knee; I definitely broke something. There is no doubt that I would have fallen if it hadn't been such an inhumanly firm grip.

Despite the pain, I swung my sword. Looking down, I saw the bone-white skin of a wight and felt the horrible despair of its touch. Through the fog of pain in my mind, I hacked at the hand and arm, but to no avail.

I recalled the stories from my elders about this creature, a *wight*.

It represented pure evil and malice; a wicked grin spread across its face as it held me fast.

Its eyes burned with a malevolence and hatred that was almost palpable. These creatures were a twisted version of their formerly human selves. With sharp, jagged needles for teeth and desiccated, leathery flesh pulled taut over bones and muscle, they were terrifying to behold.

Now, I was looking down into the eyes of a real one.

With its other hand, it started to pull itself out of its grave. Its nails were two-inch-long talons that had already sunk into my flesh, and I could feel the blood where they were embedded in my leg.

Unlike zombies and ghouls, these evil creatures were only vulnerable to magic or enchanted weapons. The wight was impervious to damage from non-magical weapons; my sword struck its arm repeatedly in futility. Even now, I could feel its frozen grip draining my life force as my leg burned in agony. At least I would soon join Darrow...

CRACK!

Thunder clapped as lightning flashed through the sky, and a cold rain began to fall. Everything had suddenly darkened, almost as if night had come early.

I could see the other undead approaching; I was surrounded. Not that it mattered since there was no way to escape the wight's grasp.

For a moment, I felt disassociated.

At least I feel calm as my end is arriving.

The pain in my leg was unbelievable as I saw the light.

The end of life is often accompanied by tales of the soon-departed seeing the tunnel of light, which hopefully leads to a life eternal in heaven...

Wait, this light is real!

HISS!

The wight let go with an inhuman hiss as a flash of light hit it dead center in the chest; it was fully halfway out of its grave now.

HISS!

Its body burst into flames from another concentrated blast of sunlight.

A *Sunbolt!*

I had heard of this magic spell, one that shot out a ray of sunlight so powerful it would burn everything in its path, especially the undead.

Not taking my new respite for granted, I ran with a speed I didn't know I had.

As I cut through the arms of the undead reaching for me, I neared the cemetery's edge. Bolts of light continued flashing from the tree line as I ran. Each was into one of the undead that had almost reached me. Without whoever was helping me, I would never make it out of this graveyard alive.

A final ghoul stood in my way.

With all my remaining strength, I swung my sword; its head fell to the ground.

Running at full sprint, I dove over the low fence of the graveyard. Tumbling and rolling, I got back to my feet. The sudden flash of pain nearly knocked me out; my leg ached horribly, but I was running for my life. Without looking back at the horde of undead, I pressed on toward the glowing light in the forest.

CHAPTER 2

ARGENT THE UNICORN

*T*he thunderclouds moved in far too quickly; something was amiss. Also, I could feel evil coming from the ancient graveyard outside my forest...

Trotting to the forest's edge, I looked out over the graveyard. I had known, even as a young foal, not to tread there.

Like an ordinary horse, we mature from infancy to maturity. Unlike them, when we arrived at maturity, we stopped aging.

I have lived for over a century in these woods. Not that I had not forayed to other lands, I had, but this was always my home. Another power of a Unicorn is that, once a day, I can *Warp* to my home forest from anywhere on Yrth. I rarely did, though, as I loved to explore and learn. Often, I would have to change into a human to keep my true identity a secret.

Ironically, I could innately cast *Beast Summoning* and

often summoned a wild horse to ride. I never forced it to help, but always asked for its consent. So far, every horse has agreed.

Over time, I learned skills as both a unicorn and a human woman. I learned much from humans and was fascinated by them. They were capable of such passion. Fortunately, they were capable of great good, but unfortunately, they were also capable of great evil. They were one to observe cautiously...

I thought again of my ancestors and the knowledge of the ages they handed down to me. This graveyard was not only where the warriors of a long-ago battle had gone for eternal slumber, but it was also the site of the very battle that took their lives.

The Battle of Amarok took place here centuries ago. The fable of Amarok tells of a mighty mage who once threatened the land—a necromancer of incredible power. He took up residence in the mausoleum located in the graveyard. Eventually, the people had had enough, and with the help of a warrior, Prince Wilhelm, they attacked the very grounds where the cemetery stands today. The forces of Wilhelm and Vzerie were ultimately both defeated in the Battle of Amarok, the name this land bore long ago. Although the warriors were buried in the very same graveyard where they fell, no one dared to enter the mausoleum. Over time, many evil creatures were drawn to the location because of its unmistakably evil aura. The townspeople gradually learned to shun the area completely.

My reverie ended as I heard a human scream. It was long and full of unimaginable agony.

No good could be happening in that graveyard, and I was worried about what was occurring.

As I watched from the forest's edge, I saw a young woman running for her life. She stopped abruptly and painfully as something grabbed her from an unsettled grave. I could see its large, bone-white upper body from here, and it had her ankle firmly in its grasp. She screamed in pain and hit it over and over with her sword.

It had no effect.

Had this been a zombie, ghoul, or ghast—she would have been effective with her strikes. However, this was a wight, a formidable undead monster with a deathly touch. Soon, she would perish, as her sword proved ineffective against it; only powerful magic and enchanted weapons could harm it. Steadying my vision, I lowered my horn as my entire body radiated with the luminosity of the sun.

There was a brilliant flash as a bolt of sunlight shot from my horn and into the wight. It hissed in agony and released the woman, but I continued attacking until it burst into flames. She was running for the forest's edge but would never make it in time. The other undead had taken the time, while she was being held, to finish surrounding her. A legion of skeletons, zombies, ghouls, and ghasts was moving in on her. I picked the ones between her and me and started hitting them with more *Sunbolts*.

I could see her long, curly red hair flowing wildly behind her as she hobbled into a run. Even from here, I could tell her leg had been severely injured by the weight. It's amazing what the fear of death can do; she was still running quite fast.

The last ghoul stood in her way as she hit it with her sword, its head cut neatly from its shoulders. She dived over the low perimeter fencing and made her way toward me.

I could make out her features now. She had fair skin but was tanned, with wide-open, terrified green eyes.

The undead did not follow. They must be limited by either command or the edge of the graveyard; I knew not which.

The mystery woman, who appeared to be in her late teens, entered the forest and headed toward me. As the glow from my body started fading, she lowered her hand from shielding her eyes and saw me fully for the first time. She covered her mouth and gasped!

"Oh my God, you are… You are a…"

There was a pause as she sensed my presence in her mind. I possessed innate telepathic abilities and reached out to her. She did not resist, allowing us to communicate at the speed of thought—

"A unicorn, yes. My name is Argent." I finished for her.

She composed herself, then suddenly remembered her flight and worriedly looked behind her.

"They did not follow," I told her.

Turning back to me again, she spoke aloud.

Although I spoke directly into her mind, she was used to physically talking—a hard habit to break.

"Thank you, Argent. You saved my life," she said.

"I am honored to do so. Who are you?"

"Sorry, I am Graciela or just Grace to my friends—"

"Owww!" she yelled.

She fell hard as her leg gave out. Adrenaline had carried her, but as it wore off, her crippled leg defeated her. She landed hard and stared at it in shock.

Leaning down, she pulled off her boot without unlacing it. A shriveled and blackened lower leg and foot greeted her. She turned to me to say something, but was unable to speak as she turned extremely pale.

"You are going into shock; lie back and stay still," I commanded.

She did, and moments later, she fell unconscious.

I walked over to her and bent my front legs under me. Leaning down close to her leg, I cried a few tears onto it. Then, I waited for her to regain consciousness. A few minutes went by, and then she groggily came to. She was muttering and not fully awake, but it would have to do. I did not want to be out here come nightfall. Although I could see well at night, I knew she could not. Plus, the undead would be emboldened come nightfall—that is their element.

So, I knelt next to her and nudged her with my snout until she grasped my silver mane and pulled herself onto my back.

With her knees straddling my back and holding

onto my mane, I carefully walked us through the forest toward the village of Greenlove…

* * *

I watched the townsfolk warily from the forest's edge. Although most know, or should know, that a unicorn is the embodiment of good, I did not trust humans always to make the correct deductions.

The village of Greenlove was a peaceful place, and people there got by on hard work. They were respectful of the forest and only hunted the animals they needed for food.

I had never been there before.

Strange to think, but I didn't want to mingle with humans so close to where I live. That would not be a good way to keep my true identity a secret.

It seems I might have to now. The woman with me would be OK, but the village would not. If she even knew the danger coming, she may not be well enough to tell them in time…

Using my hooves, I scraped leaves until I made a small pile on the forest floor. Then, kneeling once more, I leaned until Grace fell into the pile. She moaned and stirred but did not awaken.

I felt a glow as I transformed into my human form.

Magic is a strange and wonderful thing. The items I carried and wore as a human changed with me as I turned into a unicorn and returned when I changed back. No one, not even the mightiest mages, has ever understood how this innate magic works; it is a mystery that all unicorns share.

We are incredibly rare creatures—so rare that we are spoken of as a fable, a myth, a legend...

I went to put her boot back on, but it was shredded; the wight had destroyed it along with her leg.

So, instead, I put an arm under Grace and helped her to her feet. She was semi-conscious and could walk with my assistance, albeit with a limp. Looking down at her now bootless foot, I could see that the color had returned, and it looked almost normal again—my unicorn tears were healing her. As we walked from the edge of my home, Hallowdale Forest, I could see the village in the distance. Looking at the sky, I could see we would make it well before nightfall.

Minutes later, as we neared, the village guard spotted us and yelled out.

"Hail, who art thou?"

"I am Argent, and this woman—Grace—was attacked and needs aid and shelter," I replied.

The guard, in full armor, came over to me.

"Oh my, that *is* Graciela," he said.

"Yes. A wight attacked her."

His features went pale with fear.

"A wight? Please say you are having a laugh and not serious."

"I am sure. The graveyard has been disturbed, and the undead are restless now."

He nodded and said, "Bring her this way; I am taking you to the elders post-haste."

"Prepare the defenses; the graveyard is awake," he told the other guards as we passed them.

"Aye, Captain. Aye."

I looked over at him. He was a large White man, muscular and fit, and wearing the finest mail of the village—a combination of plate steel and chainmail. He carried a large ax and bow.

He looked back at me with wariness, but there was a kindness to his eyes. I could feel he was a creature of good...

"I am Captain Theodus. Thank you for saving Graciela," he said as we walked past the shocked townspeople.

"In here," he said.

We had arrived at a central building, clearly the town seat. As we entered, several people looked at us, and then a few rushed over to help Graciela.

"She must see the apothecary at once," commanded Captain Theodus.

"Yes, Captain," they said, taking her under the arm and helping her out the door.

I watched them leave...

A man in the elegant robes of a town elder approached me. He was an older Black man who looked intelligent and wise. He had long, flowing, meticulously trimmed white hair—and an equally kempt, long white beard. His hazel eyes revealed a keen intelligence. Standing quite tall at about 19 hands and fit for his age, he moved with a grace that was unusual for someone of his years.

"I am Clestus, the town's mayor and lead elder," he said.

His look told me he expected a name in return.

"Argent," I responded simply.

With a nod, he continued.

"So, please, have a seat and tell me what occurred to cause our Graciela such harm."

Taking his advice, I sat at the table as a woman came to me and poured me mead.

"G'day, Lady Argent. I am Gretchen. Thank you for saving my daughter." She hugged me and then hurried off.

I turned back to Mayor Clestus—

"I heard a commotion from the forest's edge and saw Grace being attacked by a legion of undead," I began...

As I told my tale, leaving out the part about me being a unicorn, all present went from shock to open fear. By the time my story was finished, it seemed half the village was packed into the room.

"Oh no. We have all heard the stories of Amarok but thought it was just a fanciful legend and myth," Clestus said.

"It is true, not myth."

"You sound assured?" he questioned.

"I am; I know of the legend as well. However, I do not know why they have chosen now to crawl from their graves."

Of course, I had not yet mentioned what I found in one of her bags as she lay unconscious...

With a nod, he turned to the other elders.

"What are we to do?" asked one of them.

"As always, we do what we must. Captain Theodus: I want the town guard on full alert tonight. Gretchen, turn off the taps," Clestus told the assembled room.

There was some audible grumbling from the assembled town folk. Part of it was from going onto full alert, and I am sure part of it was also the town being "cut off" at the bar.

It was clear that he was taking the veracity of my story at full value. There would be no more drinking tonight; all would be ready.

"Back to you—" he said, turning to address me.

"What were you doing in the forest? How did you help her escape? The ability for you both to survive that many undead seems... questionable..."

"I guess we were just lucky," I said.

He narrowed his eyes and studied me with a look that revealed his distrust of my answer. His eyes, not for the first time, gave me a thorough examination.

Although I knew I was transcendently beautiful to humans, I understood that was not his focus. With my mesmerizing blue eyes, long silver hair, and a fit and toned twenty-year-old woman's body, I knew I could have an amorous effect on people.

His gaze, however, was fixated on my armor and bracers, bow and quiver, and short sword. Indeed, he would recognize from their quality that I was no mere commoner. My weaponry and armor all had a faint glow of magic to those attuned to see such things.

Although I stood only 17 hands tall and weighed just 11 stone, I possessed an impressive amount of kit. He surely must have wondered how two lone women survived an attack by a graveyard full of the undead. Ultimately, he decided that it didn't matter.

"Thank you for saving Graciela, although I know there is more to the story. She is only known as Grace to her family and friends, so you must be one of those now," he smiled as he said it.

"It was a privilege to save her; I am glad she is alright now."

A man came over to Clestus and whispered in his ear. I watched him nod, look at me strangely, and then whisper back.

"If you will indulge me, I must ask a few more questions before I attend to the town's defenses. You are welcome in our town and are a heroine to us for saving Grace. However, I need to know more about what we face. You told Captain Theodus it was a wight that attacked Grace, is that right?"

"It is. I counted scores of skeletons, ghouls, ghasts, zombies, and more than one wight," I replied.

He was a little ashen but nodded his understanding gravely.

"We have spoken to the town's apothecary; he has told us Grace's leg is almost fully healed…"

Sitting completely still, he gazed into my eyes with the merest hint of a smile. A long silence ensued. Finally, I relented.

"Yes, I use healing magic," I said.

Nodding, he responded, "Yes, I am aware. However, our best magicians of the land could not have healed her leg as you have. *What are you?*"

And there it was.

Although I trusted these people as much as people could be trusted, being a unicorn was a closely guarded secret. Not because we were reviled but because of our magical powers. Many unicorns had been murdered for their horns and hooves. Although losing their magical powers once removed from our bodies, they still retained high levels of intrinsic mana, extremely helpful in making potions and enchanting weapons, and *power-stones*.

Mana is the force from which magic draws. It exists all around us, in the innate life force of both fatigue and health in animals, as well as a lesser, unidentifiable amount in the environment itself. The mana from the environment must be concentrated and stored through magical enchantment. This is how mages create *power-stones* like the ones I carry—made only from precious gems, as they are the only objects that can hold mana and still recharge from the environment after use. Unlike the massive amount of mana used to create them, they recharge only slowly for days or even longer.

Having the horns and hooves of a unicorn to assist a mage in enchanting was a prize that many mages would pay handsomely for...

With that in mind, I did not fear these townsfolk,

but human gossip and the wrong ears could endanger my life down the road.

"I am just a fighter-mage, a powerful one, " I lied.

He regarded me with skepticism. He might believe I was a powerful mage, perhaps, but he would not perceive me as a formidable fighter based on my appearance. Unbeknownst to him, I still possessed the damage resistance, protection from evil, and innate strength of an 85-stone unicorn. Thus, I was *far* stronger than a large man, even if I certainly did not look the part.

"Very well. We can use your abilities to defend our town tonight. Do you think the undead will attack us?"

"I think it is highly likely, yes. Especially now."

He did not hide his surprise.

"Oh? And why may that be?" He was smiling knowingly.

"Because you have surely found the crown that Grace was carrying."

He nodded.

"We have. What mischief has she brought upon us all?"

"She has the crown of Vzerie," I said simply.

Clestus did his best to hide his concern, but it was clear he *was* a scholar of the Battle of Amarok. He was aware of the great mage and self-appointed king, Vzerie.

"May the Gods have mercy on us all," he said as he rose to issue orders.

He knew we were all soon to be in a world of hurt.

Although none of the legends mentioned that Vzerie's crown possessed any powers beyond its splendor and its embodiment of necromantic magic, we understood it must be linked to the sudden return of the undead at the graveyard. Therefore, they would likely be coming here to retrieve it...

* * *

The town was on edge.

All had heard of the strange and beautiful woman who had saved Grace. They all knew of the undead that had arisen at the nearby graveyard, and all knew they desired to slay the living.

We had every able-bodied person ready for battle; no one would sleep tonight.

The town's defenses were meager at best. Typically, if we were under attack, the town elders would reach out to the local Baron for professional soldiers, but there was no way to send out a word in time. Unless someone wanted to run there at night, someone fast...

I approached Clestus, who was talking to Captain Theodus. Upon my approach, they turned to me.

"Hail, my Lady, how may we be of assistance?" the Captain said by way of greeting.

"Well, I am a fair rider and could make the Baron's by midnight, but the soldiers would not make it back before dawn..." I offered.

They looked at each other, and Clestus turned to me.

"Thank you. You have already done so much. Although I like this idea, your skills may be needed more urgently here tonight."

Instead, he turned to Captain Theodus, "Captain, send two riders out now to alert the Baron and request soldiers."

"Yes, Mayor," he said, turning to carry out his orders.

I nodded. It was settled then; I would be staying to help them fight, as a human.

"How is Grace?" I asked.

"She is awake now and asked to see you," Mayor Clestus said.

I nodded, "If I may have your leave, then?"

He bowed slightly, "Of course."

I turned and wandered off to find the Apothecary.

As I walked through town, sullen faces greeted me. No one thought my tale was a fallacy or untrue, so they were justifiably terrified. It is one thing to fight men and another altogether to fight the undead. Up ahead, I saw my destination. As I walked in, a gaunt man and his gaunt wife looked up and smiled.

"You must be Argent; we are honored to meet Grace's savior!"

I shook their proffered hands and sat.

"Hi, Argent," Grace said, entering the room.

Her limp had disappeared, and her color was back. She appeared to be alright now.

"I don't know your magic, but it is beyond anything we have ever seen," the gaunt man said.

A sudden look flashed onto his face.

"Oh, my manners! I am Lucero, and this is my wife, Helena," he said.

"Pleasure to meet you both. Thank you for caring for Grace," I replied.

They nodded.

I looked at Grace and saw she had on new leather boots; she saw my look.

"Yeah, my mom, Gretchen, and I wear the same size. Lucky, I must say."

She came forward suddenly and hugged me—a deep, heartfelt hug.

"Thank you so much. I would have perished without you," she whispered in my ear.

"It is what I do. Please do not share my true nature, OK?" I whispered back.

She nodded yes as she stepped away.

The gaunt couple were smiling, and Helena was now bringing in hot mugs of tea, honey, and milk for us all. We sat and drank. Meanwhile, outside the window, we could see the dimming light as the sun neared the horizon. It would not be long now...

We all sat sullenly, with the unspoken heavy in the air.

The night was almost upon us.

I looked at Helena and then spoke as I stood, "If you have any healing potions left, Grace and I could use some."

She nodded and went to get them. Returning, she handed us each two.

"These are the last we have. All the others are with the town guard; I am sorry," Helena said.

"Don't feel that way; that is where they are needed. You are a wonderful couple and the backbone of this town's health. Thank you."

They smiled at the compliment; then I turned to Grace next.

"It is time; let's go reinforce the perimeter with the guards, yes?"

She nodded yes, finished her drink, and stood up. Nothing more needed to be said as we headed out to the town's low wall. I didn't ask her if she would be fighting, because I knew she would not be deterred from aiding in the village's defense. Besides, every able-bodied person was helping tonight.

The other guards saw us as we approached. Although all of the village's walls were being manned, the wall facing the forest's edge, where the undead would probably come from, was triple-manned. The attack would probably be here. Part of me still hoped we had prepared for a quiet night and nothing would happen; I highly doubted it, though.

We walked up the steps to look out over the low wall.

Like most medieval towns, the village was surrounded by a ten-foot wall topped with spikes. It was built from heavy timber and stone, with buttressing behind it to keep it steady against a crush of invaders or a small siege device. Unlike a castle, though, it was far from impenetrable, so the undead would assuredly fight their way through. Still, it would slow them down, allowing us to whittle down their numbers before they breached it.

Dotted along the top of the protective wall were burning braziers, providing not only light and warmth but also igniting arrow tips soaked in oil. I drew my bow next to Grace, who already had hers drawn.

All was still as the sun dipped below the horizon, casting the land into darkness.

Time passed, and nothing occurred. I noticed some guards beginning to relax a bit. The metal on the soldiers' armor glinted in the light of the full moon, and the air was still. I could hear the sounds of nature as the insects and nocturnal animals moved about.

Then, one by one, the nature sounds fell silent—*they were here.*

A low crunching sound started coming from the forest. It was faint at first, but it is now building in volume. It was the sound of shambling walkers in the forest, and there were *a lot* of them.

"Archers ready!" yelled Captain Theodus.

Grace and I notched our bows and waited as archers lit their arrows.

The first ones came at a shambling run as they cleared the forest's edge.

"Fire!" he yelled.

Twang—whoosh

The first volley of fiery arrows flew toward the undead. Although several fell, more came behind them. The first ones were the zombies and ghouls.

"Fire at will!" yelled Captain Theodus again.

More arrows made a steady stream of noise as wave after wave launched.

I didn't have time to watch their accuracy as I was busy with my bow.

Notching arrows as fast as I could, I aimed and let fly...

My first target, a ghoul, took an arrow to the chest and fell. As did the next and the next.

Luckily, my quiver was a magical *Cornucopia of Arrows*, so it would never run out. It was obviously magical unless an archer only wanted to carry a tiny quiver with a single arrow...

As soon as I pulled out an arrow, another appeared in the quiver. The other soldiers, of course, did not have this luxury. Not that it mattered much; the first wave of undead had arrived at the wall. The soldiers in front dropped their bows and began using polearms to attack the nearest foes while the others continued firing arrows. I heard a scream as a man was yanked from the wall; a mass of ghouls, ghasts, skeletons, and zombies were piling into a section of the wall. Even as they fell, the heap against the wall grew; they would soon be inside.

Looking out, I could see more waves of undead, including the quick, loping gait of wights.

This was going to be an ugly fight.

My arrows were fired from a magical bow, so they still took down the wights, but the soldiers' arrows did nothing to them, so I concentrated my fire on them.

Then, the horror became worse.

A low, plaintive moan emanated from the forest as wraiths began to manifest. Like a shadow of a man on a wall but with glowing red eyes, they embodied the darkest abyss in humanoid form. Only magic could harm them, and they bore the same deathly touch as the wights.

I fired arrow after arrow, but there were too many. Soldiers yelled and screamed as the undead breached the wall. Worse still, the wraiths were almost upon us as well. No one was shooting arrows at the skeletons, as only a lucky headshot could take one down. Their bones were vulnerable to crushing attacks, but impaling ones had almost no impact on them.

Several undead had now passed the wall and entered the town. Women and children were fighting them and falling in large numbers.

I knew we were losing.

With no more options, I leaped from the wall to land on the ground below. Several undead saw me and headed my way.

FLASH

The undead near me ran in terror as I changed into a unicorn; the sunlight blasting from me in all directions, combined with my *Protection from Evil* aura, was too much for them to bear.

Scuff, scuff

My hooves pounded the ground as I sprinted away. Tucking my head down and unleashing a steady stream of low-powered *Sunbolts*, I raced along the perimeter at top speed. Those not struck by the *Sunbolts* met my golden horn, which burned like the sun and obliterated every undead it touched.

I was now bleeding profusely, but I couldn't stop. Several skeletons struck me with melee weapons as I maneuvered through the phalanx of the undead; luckily, my innate damage resistance was even more remarkable against evil...

The undead not hit by my *Sunbolts* or my horn were crushed beneath my hooves. My hooves and horn, like the rest of me, were magical. Even the 85 stones of my body weight proved dangerous to them; several skeletons shattered as my body slammed into them while I continued to run alongside the village wall. If I were not so resistant to *Death Touch*, the wights and wraiths would have been my undoing. As it was, I was tiring, and I knew it.

They didn't, though.

As soon as I made it through them and into the clear, I circled back to face them. Firing *Sunbolt* after *Sunbolt*, I kept going. I was severely hurt and could not do another sprint attack—or I would fall. Still, it had turned the tide.

BLARR!

I heard the unmistakable sound of a war trumpet from the forest.

The undead, the ones still outside the wall, turned and ran back into the forest. Each one that made it was one we would probably meet again, so I continued shooting them as they mounted a retreat.

As the last of them headed back into the forest, I heard the final twangs of bows being shot.

Except for the mournful wails for those lost and the screaming of the injured, the battlefield was suddenly quiet again.

I slowly limped to the main gate. Blood drenched my beautiful white hair, matting it in several places. Blood also leaked from my face and dripped from my snout, and the front of me was a patchwork of deep slashes from weapons and impacts from the undead. Already, I was beginning to heal, albeit slowly.

The gates opened, and several soldiers stared at me wide-eyed.

As soon as I got inside, I started walking over to the wounded. The healing potions had come out for those who were still able to receive them, but many were beyond the realm of the living now.

Too many.

My unicorn tears and spells helped to heal several of the gravely and mortally wounded, but the exertion and damage were starting to take their toll on me. Painfully limping to the center of an open area, I healed one more mortally wounded soldier.

If only I could heal just *one* more…

PART II

HALLOWDALE FOREST

CHAPTER 3

Sunlight.
I could feel its warmth on my body, and felt several hands stroking my hair and mane. Slowly, my eyelids opened. Grace, Lucero, and Helena were with me.

We had survived the night, but how many had we lost?

Lying on my side, I lifted my head and gazed at them. They were all smiling sweetly. I could smell the ointment the apothecary had used, and they had cleaned and groomed me while I was unconscious.

I gave a short whinny and, after they stepped back, I stood shakily. I had been badly injured, but my innate regeneration had healed me, along with their tinctures and salves. Once standing, I felt Grace hugging my snout and face; I gave her a lick, and she giggled.

Snort, Snort

I backed up a bit and, in a flash of light, was back to being Argent the human again.

"Welcome back, Argent. Is it still Argent, regardless of form?" Helena asked.

"It is; my name does not change," I answered.

She nodded in affirmation.

"We were worried about you there for a bit," added Lucero.

"How many?" I asked, changing the subject.

I didn't want to know, but I had to.

"We lost 87 people last night, with another 64 still badly wounded," Lucero said.

"And we would have lost everyone if not for you! I have never seen the like... heavens be praised for sending you!" Helena gushed.

I have never been good at compliments, especially when there were so many that I *didn't* save. So, I just nodded.

"I'm glad you're awake, too. We owe you a debt of gratitude—one we can never repay, Argent the unicorn," I heard a man say.

Turning, I saw that Mayor Clestus and Captain Theodus had arrived. Clestus is the one who had spoken.

"We understand your caution as we, too, have heard the tales of scalpers and poachers seeking unicorns. Your secret will always be safe in this town. I have ensured that no one speaks of your identity outside of the villagers," Clestus added.

"Thank you for that, kind Mayor, but I know it can never last; word will get out," I replied.

He nodded.

"We will do our best, but you are probably right. I cannot thank you enough, though. We may not have turned back the undead without your assistance. Henceforth, the town has bestowed upon you a new title: The Heroine of Greenlove. Whatever we have to offer is yours to take," he said, slightly bowing his head.

"Thank you. Love and protect one another when I am gone; that is all the spoils I need."

He shook my hand and gave me a gentle hug.

"I am sorry to have to ask this... However, we are forming a war party and could use your help," he looked at me imploringly.

I knew what he wanted and could not say no. Although we had the crown, it was not as simple as just returning it. We had awakened the restless dead, and they would not stop until whoever led them was put to rest again. I silently prayed it was not Vzerie, but time would tell.

"We all know that the war trumpet we heard signaled a retreat, but there are *thousands* buried in that graveyard. Last night was merely a test of our defenses; many more of them are out there, and worse, they have a leader," he said.

"Most of the soldiers must stay to defend the town, but I am putting together a small group to enter the graveyard, find whomever or whatever is leading them, and put them down. Can I count you in? I realize it is—"

"I am in, Clestus," I interrupted.

He paused.

"Very well. Thank you again. You are a godsend, Lady Argent, truly," he said, shaking my hand.

"Can you meet us all in the tavern in an hour?" he asked.

"I will be there, Mayor."

He nodded, turned, and left; the Captain, however, stayed.

"I, and the entire village's guard, are forever in your debt. Tell us what your party requires, and you shall have it."

"Thank you, Captain. I request the usual provisions for several days of travel, even if the graveyard typically requires less than one, as our journey may have... complications. Additionally, please include supplies for climbing and exploring a dungeon—everything the adventurers request that you have available." I replied.

"It will be done," he said.

He shook my hand and left. I watched him go and then turned to the apothecaries who had helped us.

"Well, I know there are many who still need your attention, Lucero and Helena. Grace and I will take our leave," I said.

"May Herates guide you," Helena said.

Herates was the god of healing and eternal summer, an everyday god worshipped by many healers.

They clapped my shoulders as we left, and Grace and I made our way to the pub.

"I guess the unicorn is out of the bag," Grace said with a chuckle.

"I suppose so," I replied with a smile.

Everyone in town waved and greeted us as we walked the rest of the way. She had either been uninjured in the battle last night or, more likely, healed while I was unconscious. As we approached the One-Eyed Lemur, she stopped and turned to me.

"No matter how this turns out for us all, I want you to know I will never forget what you have done for us. Never!"

She hugged me warmly, and we shared a smile. She was attractive, with tanned skin, freckles, and long, curvy red hair. Her eyes were the deepest green I had ever seen—like beautiful emeralds. Also, from what I observed yesterday, she possessed skill with both her sword and her bow. I knew she would be joining the war party, so I understood better than to ask. I was genuinely glad she would be coming; she would make a great warrior on our side.

As the doors swung open, we saw several men sitting around a table. The kegs were open again, and several tankards were about the table. I noticed two were poured and placed in front of two empty chairs at the table.

"For us? You shouldn't have…" Grace quipped.

Laughter.

What a lovely sound after so much suffering.

The men stood to greet us.

"Me Lady Argent, me Lady Graciela, thank ye for joining our quest," said a large dwarf wielding a battle ax almost as big as he was.

He was incredibly muscular, like a molossus war dog, with long, unkempt red hair and beard. Tall for a dwarf at about 15 hands in height, he must weigh at least 16 stone without armor. His heavy plate steel armor bore visible dents and scars, indicating he was no stranger to battle.

"Just Grace to my friends, and you are all my friends now," Grace responded.

"Aye, that we be," he replied, smiling.

"I be Drek, the Stout," he finished with a flourishing bow.

"And I am Shivalt," said a man with the distinctive pointed ears of an elf. He stood tall at approximately 18 hands, muscular yet slender. With piercing blue eyes, fair skin, and long blonde hair, he was remarkably handsome. Although he appeared to be only twenty, his actual age was likely much greater, as elves age extremely slowly after reaching maturity. His elven chainmail displayed the characteristic sheen of magic, as did his longbow and bastard sword. He wore tasteful yet expensive jewelry—no doubt enchanted with magic as well.

I noticed Grace eyeing him with more than just a casual interest...

On the other end of the looks spectrum stood a short

and rather unappealing halfling. At only 13 hands tall and weighing perhaps seven stones on a good day, he wore a scowl; I would soon learn that this was merely his default expression. He had shoulder-length, stringy black hair, brown eyes, and pockmarked skin. Clad in light leather armor, he was armed only with a dagger and a sling. I had noticed him spitting into a spittoon when I entered; he likely chewed the Zebatca leaf. Many folks partook of it; it was a mild stimulant and mostly harmless.

"Hail, fair maidens! I am known as 'Toad,'" he said sheepishly.

"Honored to meet you, 'Toad, '" I said, extending my hand.

His face turned bright red, and he cast his glance down as he gently shook my hand.

"Aye, I thinks you make Herbert shy…" said Drek.

"Just Toad, please," Herbert/Toad replied to Drek.

"Toad it is—a pleasure," I said.

We took a moment to all sit and enjoy our tankards when the Lemur's door opened, and Mayor Clestus entered. I must admit I was taken aback.

He no longer wore the elegant robes of a town elder; he revealed his true vocation—that of a mage.

His gray robes boasted pockets galore, and many strange and wonderful artifacts hung from his wide cloth belt and tunic. He wore a peculiar type of hat, almost like a fedora but taller. Like the elf, he adorned himself with magical jewelry. He possessed a long white wooden staff with a large red jewel embedded at its end. The staff was sturdy and could inflict considerable damage if swung in battle.

"You already know me; I am *Mage* Clestus," he said simply.

"Aye, ye high smugness, have a tankard to fill thee hole in yer face," Drek said to him.

We all chuckled as Clestus sat.

The pub's owner, Gretchen, brought another tankard and placed it before him.

Clestus eyed Drek and raised his pint,

"To our success," he toasted.

"To success," we all said, taking a swig of beer...

* * *

VZERIE

I AROSE from the slumber of eons.

Someone must have worn my crown.

Indeed, I could always count on humans to do the wrong thing and to give in to their greed.

A harsh cackling emanated from my desiccated throat. Whoever wore that crown would have been afflicted by the powerful *Rotting Death* spell imbued upon it. Needless to say, my crown would not affect the unliving...

I remained in my inanimate state until someone was foolish enough to enter the graveyard. The crown was close enough to the mausoleum that its *Lesser Gaes* spell would affect anyone who touched it. The spell would compel them to pick it up and wear it on their head, awakening me from my slumber.

Their bodily death would transfer the life force that was needed to reanimate my doppelganger.

I planned to win the battle against Prince Wilhelm, of course, as I had only made the crown in case I fell in battle. Then, its spell would make a hapless soldier pick it up and wear it, but luck was not with me. As I cast my final spell to kill Prince Wilhelm, his magical sword decapitated me.

As all who fought perished in the end, there was no one left to wear the crown.

So then, as the ages went by, the crown must have become hidden. Luckily, it was found.

After so long away, I rose silently from where I lay, entombed deep in the labyrinth of my own design.

I had filled my tomb with traps—both magical and mundane—but now I could add undead to the monsters that had already found it and called it home. There were lands above to conquer and people to subjugate, but first, I had to make ready...

As I began to assemble things for more potent spells and wards, I thought of what may be out there. What had happened since the Battle of Amorak? To me, it had just occurred. However, I knew a great deal of time must have passed. I could see the significant aging of some of my magical ingredients and of the room I was in. Much time had passed, although it was of no consequence to me, for I could live almost forever.

Most of my spells could be cast at a mere glance, but

the most potent took time and resources to create. I cherished the years that some spells took to develop.

I wonder who will be coming to my lair this time?

Pondering this, I began creating *Invisible Wizard Eyes* to send out. Each is made from the eyeball of a dead creature. Unfortunately, most of the eyes in my jars had lost their magical protection and rotted away. A few were still usable, however. Imbued with magic, they would fan out into the tomb and the forest beyond. My eagerness to see what had transpired filled me with yearning.

My love of learning *all* things had made me a monster to others.

The only desire I had was to learn more magic and become increasingly more powerful in return. I did not wish to become what I am; I simply did not want to face a mortal death due to disease or aging. However, the research and practice of necromancy were criminal acts in every fiefdom in the land. This crime would result in the offender being put to death, usually publicly and painfully.

Nevertheless, I was not to be deterred.

As I aged into an old wizard, I knew my time was coming to an end, but there was still so much left to learn! My final mortal spell would be to bring me everlasting "life" as an undead. It took much of my fortune to create, but in the end, I cast the ceremonial magic that took my life, changing me forever into what I am now.

Seeing my reflection in the bright sheen of a nearby shield, I took a moment to look.

My tall and frail skeletal body wore the same exquisite imperial cloak I had slumbered in, only now, it was in tatters from time and decrepitation. My withered flesh was pulled over my skeletal frame, with eyes hollowed out—empty black sockets where my eyes had long ago rotted away. Now, they were mere hollows with a crimson glow in their centers.

I am a Lich.

As I absentmindedly clawed at my cloak with my sharp, bony fingers, further tattering it, I heard a squeaking sound.

Flitting over to my shoulder was my familiar—an Imp. Standing only two hands high, it resembled nothing more than a bright red, winged demon—because it was one.

"Arubus, go forth and spread misery to any invaders. Thereafter, return to me." I commanded.

It squeaked happily and flitted off into the tomb. I was not concerned about it being alone, as it was an immortal being from the depths of hell. Although I was tied to it, its loss would only hurt me somewhat and pose no real threat. When it was near me, I felt more powerful, however. The most significant advantage of a familiar is that I could see through its eyes, and it could teleport back to me at will—its will or mine. So, if anything were to reach me, Arubus would always return to assist me. Although tiny, it could cast mighty magic, especially with the *power-stone* I had given it. Its evil was as great as mine, so it was happy to be in my service. As it fluttered off, I could see it clutching the flawless diamond in its tiny hands.

Crackle

My bones made snapping, creaking noises as I moved about the chamber.

Walking to my armory, I examined the items I would be using: several *power-stones* placed in a bag, a *Ring of Fire Resistance*, and a *Ring of Dexterity*. Also ceremonially displayed in its cradle was my most valued possession: *the Staff of the Lich*.

Even longer than my own, very tall 20 hands, the staff awaited. Weighing in at only two kilograms, it was jet-black, the color of the abyss. It was made from a mix of the bones of the violently evil dead and forged in the flames of Hades. It cast *Death Touch* on any living being whenever it struck them or was even grasped by them; no armor could stop this effect. This was the same life drain that wights, wraiths, and shadows did to their living prey. Plus, it also cast *Total Paralysis* if it touched the head or *Wither Limb* if it hit a limb. These effects, unlike *Death Touch*, could be resisted by a very strong-willed person.

I felt its deadly drain as I picked it up. Luckily, being a lich, I was not a living thing but an undead one. I could feel my dry skin creak as it pulled into a vicious smile. It was time to prepare for my next guests—I had been away for far too long…

***

ARGENT THE UNICORN

It was afternoon as we entered Hallowdale Forest.

Between soldiers requiring healing, food, and rest, we also waited for the Baron's men to arrive. He sent an initial contingent of a hundred men, but most of them would be defending our village. A small number of his best warriors would be accompanying us.

Our war party was to be a band of thirteen. The six of us were being supplemented by seven of the Baron's professional soldiers. Captain Theodus had stayed behind to command the defense and ready the village for the next nightfall.

We hoped to keep the undead concentrated on us and not the town.

My motivations were simple—to protect good from evil, that's it. No other impulse motivated me; it was innate to our species to do so. Sure, additional magical treasure could aid me and be welcome, but that was not the impetus for my actions. Greed was not in my nature as a unicorn.

That was the curse of being a humanoid.

All the humanoid races, whether half-orcs, dwarves, or humans, felt greed. I pitied them.

As we entered the forest that afternoon, I had the lead, as I was intimately familiar with every foot of the forest we had just entered. No longer fearing discovery by my current company, I changed back into a unicorn so that Grace could ride on me. The town guards with us were sworn to secrecy.

My capacity to resist damage and mind control against evil was shared with those nearby. Additionally, she would possess the advantage of a commanding view and quick movement to assist her in combat.

As I walked, it was strange to see the gloom that had descended on my beautiful forest. The trees, already adept at filtering out much of the sun's light, now only let the diffuse, overcast sky limited ingress to our eyes, making for a gloomy, haunted feel that did not make me happy. It was not just the earth they had poisoned with their arrival, but the sky as well.

Sensing evil ahead, I stopped and whinnied.

Gesturing with my head by making three thrusts to our front left, I let my party know where I had detected the enemy.

They formed a circle around me and readied ranged weapons. Grace dismounted quickly with an acrobatic leap. Drek had a slew of small throwing axes, Toad had a sling, whilst Grace and Shivalt had readied their bows. Clestus and I would be using magic. I noticed Clestus was already casting spells to support the team's defenses, what they called "buffing" spells.

We did not wait long.

Something massive was moving through the forest, crushing tree branches and brambles alike. With a crack, it broke through the trees and into view. Standing almost 40 hands tall, it was over twice the height of a man. With long, ungainly arms and legs and bony, scaly, mottled green skin, it looked at us. Its short, stringy black hair reminded me of Toad's, except that it writhed on its own as if it were alive. Its dull, all-black eyes glowered with evil intent. Long, sharp fingers splayed from broad, giant hands, and it smiled a wicked grin as it broke into a ground-eating, loping gait toward us.

It was a Giant Troll.

Twang!

Several arrows, a hand-axe, and a sling bullet zipped its way.

HAARGH!

It let out a terrifying yell as it charged.

There were many hits and a few misses. I could see where some of the arrows penetrated its thick, scaly hide, but others bounced off. Meanwhile, the small fiery explosion from Toad's *fire-stone* did seem to hurt it—

I lowered my horn...

The seven town guards and Drek rushed forward to meet it as it closed. Hacking with blades and Drek's giant axe, they surrounded it. I saw it slash an arm out, and its giant bony hand ripped away a town guard's shield, his hand and arm flying off with it.

AHH!

The man screamed and fell as blood pulsed out from where his arm once was.

THUD

Drek hit it dead in the stomach and sunk deep. Black, viscous blood shot out.

HAARGH!

It swiped at him, but he jumped aside with surprising alacrity.

More blades bit into the troll, but none seemed to do much harm. To make things worse, the axe wound was already starting to heal.

WHOOSH—BOOM

I felt the heat as Clestus fired an *Explosive Fireball* into it. The ball exploded on its chest, and it screamed out again.

That hurt it!

Concentrating, I let loose a *Sunbolt* from my horn, but it sidestepped right as I did. Instead, my blast alighted a tree behind it.

Its elongated face, with a comically large nose, snapped forward onto a guard's head, and he screamed as it bit down. His now headless body fell to the blood-soaked earth, as the troll swallowed his head, metal helm and all.

I let loose another *Sunbolt* from my horn, this time striking the troll's torso. There was a loud hiss as it burned a hole like a giant hot coal into it. A large area was now blackened, and I could see that it was not healing. Another fireball hit a leg and charred it badly. It was good to see that my *Sunbolt* and Clestus's *Explosive Fireballs* were harming it, but all the non-magical weapons had little effect upon it.

Drek's axe was magical and inflicting damage, but

only Clestus' and my attacks did not heal. This monster regenerated at an alarming rate! Drek's strike to its torso was now barely visible on its warty, mottled-green skin.

HAARGH!

I saw an eye socket explode in a small ball of fire, and the eye launched out onto the ground; it seemed that Toad had more magical stones to shoot from his sling. The eye socket was smoking and charred, but the eyeball on the ground had grown tiny feet and was running back toward the troll.

The troll surged forward and struck another guard, flinging him violently into a tree and killing him. Grace was firing her bow as quickly as she could, but since her arrows were not magical, they were popping back out of the troll by the time the next one hit. The troll regenerated much faster than the legends described.

Another *Sunbolt* and *Fireball* hit it. Its whole torso was now blackened, and my last strike had given it a pronounced limp that slowed its attacks. Drek cut one of its arms off at the elbow. They hacked and hacked, trying to kill it.

"Look out!" Grace screamed at Drek.

The warning was not in time.

The troll's disembodied arm had crawled by its fingers and had grabbed his ankle. He yelled out in pain as it squeezed. Drek's axe bit down hard, just above the troll's wrist, severing it in two.

But the hand kept squeezing.

AHH!

Drek fell as his leg gave out. Sensing its opportunity, it began crawling up his body toward his neck. A quick-thinking Toad saved his life. As it crawled—much faster than I thought possible—toward his throat, it exploded into a shower of fiery bits; another hit from Toad's *firestones* launched from his sling.

AHH!

Drek cried out and lay still. The fiery explosion had killed the troll's hand, but it also knocked Drek out.

The troll was slowing and seemed to be getting confused. Every time a fighter hit it, it had to turn to one that had got behind it. To add to its confusion, Clestus finally got a great headshot, and it was running around with its hair on fire now—literally.

It swung madly and blindly out towards its attackers.

Seeing my chance, I sprinted at it.

Hearing my whinnying, the guards between me and it made to get out of my way.

Luckily, it had turned its back on me while fighting the others and couldn't see me as I sprinted at it. Now, at full speed, I lowered my head and fired a final *Sunbolt* right before ramming my horn into it.

FZZT—WHAM!

My horn was buried deep into its back as I jumped and rammed into the troll. My momentum knocked it off its feet, and we fell, entangled, to the forest floor. There was a horrible burning meat smell as we tumbled and slammed to the earth. Yanking my head back and forth, my muscles bulged with strain. My glowing horn sizzled as it cut the troll's torso apart like a meter-long, hot paring knife. The others rushed in and held down its limbs.

There was a searing heat as Clestus used a *Flame Jet* to burn every part of it.

By the time we hunted down and killed the parts that were cut off and attacked us autonomously, we were all exhausted.

Finally, the troll was dead.

Luckily, Clestus also knew frost spells; otherwise, my beloved forest would surely be fully engulfed in flames by now.

It was time to assess the damage the troll had wreaked upon us.

We had lost two of the town guards, and I had to heal Drek with a lot of energy before he stirred and awoke. Several others were also wounded, and I rendered them aid as well. Miraculously, the one who lost his arm was also saved, although he would be out of action for a little while as he healed, even with the aid of unicorn tears. Overall, we were fortunate to have done so well. Only losing two people fighting such a horrifying creature was a mixed blessing. Never, in my century-plus of life, had I encountered its like.

What evil must have been released to draw such a hell-spawned creature into my Hallowdale Forest!

As we finished burning the last remnants of the troll to ash, we discovered our fallen guard's metal helm and a magical dagger. The dagger must have been consumed earlier, or perhaps the troll simply regenerated around it, after some unfortunate adventurer had stabbed it.

None of us questioned who should take it. Toad thanked us as he fastened the dagger's sheath to his belt. Once we ensured everyone was prepared again, we ventured farther into the forest.

CHAPTER 4

We proceeded warily through the forest. I led us by clear streams to refill our canteens and water skins, and even found us some nourishing food to eat. The clouds continued to block the sun's rays, casting long shadows through the forest. By late afternoon, we had nearly reached the other side of the forest.

I glanced over at Grace. She noticed my gaze on her bag, the one containing the evil crown. She gave me a look that conveyed her understanding of my thoughts.

How can such a small crown hold so much power?

After hearing what happened to Darrow, none of us were eager to touch the crown again, much less put it on. So, it was decided by all that the crown would stay in its bag until we concluded our mission. If it were needed, somehow, to defeat the evil, it would do so. If not, when it was all over, it would be melted down by

Micah, the village blacksmith. The gold and gems would be sold, with a split of the proceeds to Darrow's family, Graciela, and the town's coffers. It seems like the elder council worked like a town council should—to do the right and good thing.

First, though, we had to survive this adventure.

It was a pleasant walk, especially since I knew my way around the forest better than anyone else. Rarely would an evil creature venture into Hallowdale Forest. Many evil creatures could sense good the way I sensed evil, so they knew this forest was a protected place. The fact that the troll had entered was a testament to the evil power that the crown had unleashed.

We heard a rustling in the brambles, and a small furry animal emerged; it hadn't noticed us yet. Another one dashed out and tackled it. The two animals had brown fur and eyes and were actually quite adorable. They were brown bear cubs. They finished their tussle and, suddenly, they turned and saw us for the first time.

Grace took a step forward, smiling, but I stepped in front of her to stop her.

FLASH

I was back to being human again.

"Everyone, stay still," I said.

It was too late.

ROAR!

A gigantic brown bear came crashing into the clearing, no more than fifty meters from us. She saw us and reared to her full 36 hands of height. Weighing in at probably 130 stone, she was colossal. These bears are carnivorous, bad-tempered, and territorial. To make matters worse, we were near her cubs.

She dropped back to all fours and started running our way, still snarling.

Only a short distance away, she slowed suddenly and sniffed towards me.

I stepped away from the party to approach her. Instinctively, I had "cast" *Beast Soother* on the bear. If it had continued, my fellow adventurers would have had to kill her. As a result, those adorable little cubs would have lost their mother to nurture and protect them.

HUFF

As she came nearer, I could feel our connection. She looked into my eyes and slowly walked towards me. Shivalt lifted his bow, an arrow already notched; I waved at him to lower it. He did, but I could tell he was ready to lift and fire at a moment's notice.

The bear finished walking up to me. Even on all fours, we were eye to eye. She was indeed a magnificent and gigantic creature. She approached and sniffed me. Then, she nuzzled her snout against me, and I petted her. The cubs came running over as well, but the mama bear huffed at them, making them stay back. My intrinsic animal empathy and ability to soothe beasts had calmed her, but she still had a job to do—protecting her cubs. I petted her gently and reached into my *Bag of Holding*. Pulling out some berries and cured salted meat jerky, I fed the bear. She gently ate from my hand, then looked from me to her cubs and back to me again.

Her message was clear.

I carefully took out more food and placed it on the ground at my feet. Motioning to the party, we walked around where the cubs were and then doubled back to our original path. I turned back and saw all three bears contentedly eating.

I was glad I could help the bear rather than harm it. She surely would have attacked us and just as certainly been killed. Now, not only were she and her cubs safe, but they were also well-fed.

Smiling, I continued our journey. I chose to remain in human form for a while, uncertain of the reason; I guess I simply felt like it.

The far edge of the forest was close now, only half a league away, when I saw them. We had just crested a low hill and could see a small valley in the forest below. Having excellent vision and a unique knowledge of the area, I figured this might be where they would lay a trap if they were here, and sure enough—

They lay in ambush, their disguised shapes barely visible and an aura of malice palpable in the air.

"Okay, everyone, they are lying in wait up ahead. Our only route is through that valley if we want to make it to the graveyard by nightfall. They have an ambush set along one edge, with a team prepared to cut us off from behind…"

I walked over to a section of dirt and grabbed a stick. Making a diagram on the ground, I showed where the two groups of undead waited in ambush.

"This is bad. These mindless creatures could never

pull this off on their own. Something intelligent is giving the orders," Clestus said.

"Arhg, they be quick in the head, eh?" said Drek.

I continued to explain our tactics, "Yes, it appears so. Our advantage, aside from not rushing in, is that they may lack intelligence once the conflict begins. That is where our plan will come in…"

* * *

SHIVALT WAS RIDING me as I walked into the valley.

We were the "bait," and I had picked the Elf for practical reasons. He was adept at archery from horseback, and, as a unicorn, I was the most fleet of foot once the battle began. I hoped that their flank attack would assume this was the whole party, and the other group of undead would then move to cut off our rear. Unbeknownst to the rear group of undead, the rest of our party had sneaked up close behind *them*. Once the attack started, the "rear guard" of the enemy would also be attacking us. When that happened, the rest of our party would attack *that* group from behind, with the element of surprise.

We would surprise our ambushers, and we would need it.

Already, I had counted over forty on the flank and an equal number in the rear. Moreover, any wraiths, or even worse, shadows, would remain invisible until the attack. The numbers were likely much higher…

Shivalt had his magic bow out and had an arrow notched; we were ready.

One of the magical properties of a unicorn is the ability known as *Deflect Missiles*. It affected those near me as well, so Shivalt would also be protected. Although this was also a spell, mine was an innate ability possessed by all unicorns, whether in human or unicorn form. In fact, I had practiced how to parry missiles with my sword just to make it appear that it was simply my skill and luck at play, not a magical effect. Obviously, that was not possible as a unicorn.

We could not run to the side and get away, so we had to move forward—at least, that was *their* plan for us. Taking an educated guess, I assumed there would be another ambush or trap if we proceeded that way. Instead, we would break left, away from the undead assault team, toward a small area of cover I knew.

Foolishly, their leader did not consider my intimate knowledge of the forest. There was a slight depression on that side of the valley, providing some cover as we returned fire on our assailants, with Shivalt staying beside me. Not that we needed it, but I hoped they would not notice that all their shots were "misses" and would engage us that way for as long as possible. We needed to reduce their numbers before engaging them in melee. In the best-case scenario, we were outnumbered at least six to one, so we had to whittle them down first.

At a casual, wary trot, I acted like I was alert and looking all around, but we knew exactly where they were. My tactics were sound when we heard the first arrows fly.

Swoosh

A wave of arrows flew our way. We could hear them flying close by as they missed us. Whinnying, I ran for my cover as Shivalt fired arrow after arrow. If he hit anything while I was sprinting, he deserved an award.

We made it to the depression, and I butted up against the edge. Only my head was above it, and Shivalt was firing from unicornback.

Several arrows and spears came from our right. The rear guard of the enemy was attacking now as well.

With my peripheral vision, I saw some of them fall, stricken from behind. So far, none seemed to notice our saviors in their midst.

As Shivalt was notching another arrow, I concentrated. I could see the dark shadow of a wraith coming down toward us. It was not alone...

FZZT

My *Sunbolt* hit its dead center and, in a flash of light, it was gone—vaporized. The arrows and spears lessened as the first wave drew near us; so far, so good.

I snorted, and Shivalt leaped off me onto the edge of the depression, drawing his bastard sword.

FLASH

In an instant, I transformed back into a human. I pulled my sword as I rushed up the edge and stood near Shivalt. We had each other's backs now, and he knew to stay near me to be safe from the arrows and spears.

I wish I could have kept using *Sunbolt*, but that was

one thing that only the unicorn horn could do. I was pretty good with a sword, though. Adding to my skill was my magic vorpal sword, which helped guide my strikes and delivered extra damage with its impossibly sharp blade.

The first zombie reached out for me.

SWISH, SMACK

Its head plopped off as my sword went through its neck like butter. Swinging the blade again, I stopped a sword with a loud clanging of metal. Spinning, I took out the skeleton's legs and leaped aside as a large polearm smashed down where I just was.

There were too many of them.

I felt enormous pressure as one of them struck me in the chest. My armor stopped most of it, but not all. Blood was surging from the wound; I would need to heal soon…

* * *

MAGE CLESTUS

The plan was working.

I am leading the attack on the rear element. Casting buffing spells—to help the other fighters' aim and damage—I would wait on fire magic until they had discovered us.

The undead began their attack on Argent and Shivalt.

Twang

Grace fired her bow. Simultaneously, Drek threw hand axes, and Toad shot his sling. Several undead fell as they reloaded. None turned; we still had the element of surprise.

Another volley. This time, they did notice!

Several turned our way, as the others amongst them were momentarily confused; most undead are vicious but not too bright. As we engaged, some went back to shooting at Argent and Shivalt while the rest charged us. We dropped our ranged weapons and prepared for melee.

Now that the jig was up, I concentrated.

The giant red ruby on my staff glowed brightly. My staff was a *Staff of Immolation* and gave me aid and extra power when casting fire spells.

I would need it.

The first ghoul, or possibly ghast, was nearly upon me. Although they were physically identical, the ghast was more intelligent and cunning than its ghoul kin, which possessed almost no intelligence. Its mottled and decaying flesh was wrapped tight around its bones, and it had protruding, sharp teeth for rending flesh from bone...

WHOOSH—BOOM

The blast of my *Explosive Fireball* blew it apart, also knocking a couple of ghouls off their feet and alighting them. They rolled on the ground and lay still, smoking.

Drek was chopping into the undead, often cutting them in two with his giant, double-sided battle axe.

Toad was running away but dropping caltrops

behind him, causing several ghouls to develop a limp. Occasionally, he would stop to shoot his sling before running again.

I concentrated for a couple of seconds...

WHUUMPF

I had cast *Body of Flames* and was now a humanoid composed entirely of flames. As the first of the undead approached me, I cast *Fire Cloud* onto the ground at my feet.

A swirling cloud of fiery embers and flames erupted in the air for two meters around me.

Lastly, I cast a *Flame Jet* spell and maintained it just as the first ghouls, skeletons, and zombies arrived. Behind them, I could see the wights and wraiths coming. I didn't dodge their attacks while aiming the three-meter flame at the ones who had reached me. Some fell from immolation, while others disengaged while still alight. I felt their blades slash through my body to no avail.

The wraiths and wights were the worst. Even if I prioritized them, their touch would still drain me. The first wights to arrive quickly caught fire and collapsed, but I knew the wraiths were not susceptible to my flames.

Once they got close, I would have to flee.

After taking out as many enemies as I could, I broke into a sprint as the first wraiths reached me. Fortunately, we were matched in speed as I raced towards where Argent now stood, appearing as a woman instead of a unicorn. I felt arrows slice through my fiery body; I was almost to Argent. Some of the undead attacking them took notice and left the others to engage me instead. I saw that Drek and Grace were still fighting where I had left them, and the wraiths were all following me; they must have sensed my lingering vulnerability to them. I only hoped Argent and Shivalt understood that I needed their help...

* * *

ARGENT THE HUMAN

I SAW the flaming body of Clestus sprinting my way; several wraiths were in pursuit. He and the rest of the party had decimated the rear attack group, but those would not be affected by fire. I realized what Clestus was doing. As he ran past, the wraiths followed.

The first one met my blade.

Standard weapons do not harm the incorporeal. Mine was not a typical blade, however.

The magic vorpal weapon sliced it in half at the midsection. In eerie silence, it floated apart and then simply faded from view—it was destroyed. The others turned on Shivalt and me as Clestus engaged the remaining undead. His *Flame Jet* spell worked wonders on the ghouls and especially on the desiccated husks of the zombies. The skeletons, however, were less affected, as their bones were resistant to the heat of his flames.

Shivalt expertly whirled and eliminated another wraith; he was a true artist, and watching him was like observing a circus performer, except with real enemies "dying."

I saw Drek, Grace, and Toad running our way. They had dispatched the undead that made up the rear attack group. I watched as another town guard fell to a skeleton's blade buried deep into his chest. Another guard hit it with a mace, and it shattered in a spray of bones. The crushing attacks were especially effective on them, so much so that I made a practice of turning the flat of my blade against them.

As we finished off the last of them, I saw another guard fall, blood spilling from a wound in his neck. I rushed to him and placed my hands on him, hoping the others would notice my struggle and come to my aid.

They did.

I could feel the strain as I poured energy into his neck wound. First, I stopped the bleeding, and then the wound slowly healed as the sparkling from my healing spell went into him. He was still alive but unconscious.

I stood, feeling a wave of fatigue.

All was quiet again as we tended to the wounded and began to search the destroyed undead. I knew there would be nothing of intelligence value, but some might have equipment or weapons we could use.

"Argent?"

I turned; it was Toad. Although the weakest among us, his sling, especially with the *fire-stones* he wielded, did a number on the enemy. Even as he ran from them, his caltrops slowed them and took several away from our melee. He had proven immensely valuable in combat.

"Yes, Toad?"

"One of the wights had this; I thought a mage—you or Clestus—could analyze it," he said.

I looked at it and cast an *Analyze Magic* spell.

"This is a *Ring of Strength*, pretty potent also," I told him.

I smiled as he glanced around and slipped it onto his thumb.

He smiled back at me and then walked away.

After looting the bodies, we found primarily standard armor and weapons. They carried no gold or mundane treasure, but a few did have items of interest. In addition to Toad's *Ring of Strength*, there was also a *Ring of Acid Resistance* and *Boots of Dexterity*. We decided our thief could make the most use of them as well. So, Toad got all the loot this time.

The town guard I healed had lived and was now awake. Unfortunately, the blackened, shriveled husk of a wight victim and another with a sword still embedded in his chest were beyond saving. Three town guards and the rest of our party members remained capable of combat. We had walking wounded, which Clestus and I healed until they were well enough to fight again.

As we all recovered, we stayed alert for an attack, but none came. The day was growing late, and the sun was sinking closer to the horizon. Not knowing what lay ahead of the ambush, we just took a different route at the end of the valley and went around whatever awaited us. Our goal was to reach the graveyard, not clear the forest. Thus, we set out once more…

* * *

WE STUDIED the graveyard in the late rays of the sun.

It appeared as if prolific grave robbers had struck—unearthed graves stretched across the entire cemetery, and it seemed like thousands of undead had arisen. However, none were visible to the naked eye. We watched for several minutes, but in the end, none of us saw any signs of the undead present. Besides, the sun would set soon, and we wanted to be inside before then.

"OK, let's head to the mausoleum. I am betting that is where our undead leader resides," Clestus said.

No one had assigned him to be "in charge," but he possessed the unmistakable traits of a good leader, making him a suitable fit. Moreover, he *was* the town mayor…

We strode across the open field, still able to see the bodies of the slain undead from when I rescued Grace. After passing through the large, open, metal cemetery gates, we could see the undead bodies up close now.

"This was your handiwork?" Clestus asked me.

"Yes, Grace and I," I replied.

He nodded.

We checked them for loot and, finding none, continued through the cemetery. The stone gargoyles in the distance leered menacingly at us as we made our way across the vast graveyard.

I could smell the scent of pine as the wind blew mournfully through the graveyard. The sky was still overcast, with foreboding, dark thunderclouds swirling above us. I felt the unmistakable chill of evil coming from the mausoleum.

As we approached the sturdy, thick wood doors, I glanced again at the gargoyles. They glared down menacingly but remained mere statues of evil. We formed a hasty semi-circle around the door to keep guard while Toad went to work on the lock.

Several minutes went by; then we heard a click and the loud, slow creak of heavy doors opening.

The main room was large, and the walls held shelves of urns and caskets. The open floor held many more of the same. In the center was a spiral staircase that went down to the catacombs below. Behind it was a raised dais with an impossibly large casket on it.

We cautiously made our way inside. I possessed the unicorn's gift of sensing evil. Unfortunately, this place was so flooded with malevolence that it was difficult to identify any enemies in time. My senses began to scream at me; true evil was upon us.

"Be wary; evil is nigh," I said to the party.

Sure enough, just moments later, several caskets slid open as their undead occupants spilled out. A low, inhuman moan echoed from several urns as dark shapes emerged from them—Shadows.

Wraiths were terrible enough, but shadows were a

faster and more dexterous form of them, and their *death touch* was even more potent. Besides being more insubstantial than a wraith, they also did not have glowing red eyes; they were truly just shadows. Hard to see in the dark and gloom of a dungeon, but easy to see in sunlight. So, I glowed brightly with sunlight to make them visible and to drive them away. The only thing they hated more than all life was light, especially sunlight...

We quickly formed a circle, with the fighters and I on the outer perimeter and Clestus and Toad in the center.

Plink! WHOOSH—BOOM

Toad's *fire-stone* hit a ghoul as it crawled from its casket, exploding and shattering both it and the casket. Meanwhile, Clestus's *Explosive Fireball* took out a couple more of them.

The rest made their way to us.

I feigned a jab and then dropped low and spun. My sword took out a ghoul at the knees, and it fell to the ground. Another took its place. As it reached for me, I thrust my sword into its chest and yanked sideways. It dropped to the ground, destroyed.

We were surrounded yet making good headway against our foes. The shadows stayed back in the... shadows. My sunlight was keeping them at bay for now.

Then, I saw something that chilled me to the core.

On the central dais of the room stood that single

large casket. The stone lid was violently thrown off, and a vast humanoid form emerged.

It was a Wraith-Lord.

Standing at 27 hands high, it towered over a man and a half in height. Clad in plate mail as dark as night, it wielded a massive polearm with a menacing, curved blade the size of a cutlass at its end—a Naginata.

Its mouth opened, revealing a glowing maw, and it screamed—

HAAAARHG!

My natural aura of resistance to evil aided those near me, but we all had to fight off the fear its shout caused. Three of the town guards and Toad ran for the doors we came in, possessed by fear. One of the guards caught a blade on the way and fell to the floor, unmoving. Toad and the other two ran screaming into the setting sun outside.

WHOOSH—BOOM

The wraith-lord was hit dead in the chest by an *Explosive Fireball* and was knocked from its feet.

It was not out, however.

I looked away from the monster as I blocked an axe from a skeleton and quickly reversed the blade into its neck with a flat-sided downward strike. My sword came free as it fell into a pile of unenchanted bones.

Our perimeter was holding, protecting Clestus to cast more spells.

"Argent, be free!" he yelled.

He motioned from me to the wraith-lord, who had

just finished standing back up, and I felt a powerful pull. I did not resist it.

POP

I was standing behind the wraith-lord now, as Clestus had cast *Teleport Other* on me.

It was a brilliant tactical move. The undead had us surrounded, and the wraith-lord had many spells and "shouts" that it could do to us as a group, ones that did not affect the undead. If we waited to fight our way out, the monster would be free to attack us with impunity.

Without warning or mercy, I leaped forward and slashed my blade across the length of its back. My sword carried the strength of two men—because unicorns retain the strength of a horse when they transform into humans. It cut through his plate mail, and the sharp, vorpal blade nearly sliced the Wraith-lord in half. Somehow, it still lived.

Spinning with a speed that belied its size, it wrenched my sword, still lodged in it, from my grasp. With no time to dodge and no sword to parry it with, it swung its polearm at me—

I raised my arm, protected by the *Bracers of Defense*, to block it. Smacking my arm against me, it hurled me across the room. My arm was severely broken, and my body was in poor condition as well. If I hadn't parried with my arm, it would have killed me. Thankfully, I was too close for it to use the blade at the end of the polearm; otherwise, I would be dead.

My Lord, the strength of it was unbelievable!

FLASH

I was now a unicorn again, albeit one with a broken front leg. Sunlight glowed from my body.

It turned on me and brought its polearm high overhead for a killing blow.

FZZT

A blinding flash erupted from my horn, causing the weapon to fly from its grasp as my *Sunbolt* struck its arm. The smoldering stump of its severed right arm did not deter it—

HAKHATA!

It screamed out a weird yell and lifted its remaining arm.

CRACKLE!

Lightning streamed out of its arm and into my whole body.

I spasmed in pain and fell as its electricity short-circuited my ability to stand or even think. The agony was unbearable! My last thoughts were of my party; I hoped they would defeat this monster and avenge me. Through my pain, having fallen onto my side, all I could do was watch as it continued its assault. Smelling the scent of cooking meat, I felt my life ebbing away...

WHOOSH—BOOM

The crackling that filled my ears suddenly stopped as the wraith-lord's head exploded from an *Explosive Fireball*. I smiled as I gently floated into unconsciousness...

PART III

THE TOMB

CHAPTER 5

I awoke to the concerned looks of my party members.

Lifting my head, I tried to stand to no avail. My front leg was still broken, although it had a bandage now; I could feel that I was too injured and would not survive. The room was littered with the destroyed undead and piles of skeleton bones, and I could still smell cooked flesh. Undoubtedly, my own.

And there was also quite a lot of human blood on the ground as well.

Calmly, I shut my eyes and concentrated. I could feel my bones resetting and my wounds healing. My seared flesh and organs started to mend. In a few moments, I stood, wholly healed.

The others just stared in amazement.

"I had heard of such things, but I have never

witnessed them. The complete healing powers of a unicorn…" Clestus said in awe.

I reached out telepathically to Clestus, and he let me in.

"Are others in need of aid?" I asked him.

"Yes, let's heal up before we go down those stairs," he said aloud, cocking his head toward the spiral staircase that descended to the catacombs.

I saw that Toad and the other guards had returned; there was no shame in their running. A *Fear* spell was a potent thing. When it took hold, the subject was filled with an all-consuming dread that forced them to run away.

Shivalt was down and mortally wounded but still alive, so I cried my unicorn tears onto him. Moments later, he awoke, dumbfounded and wholly healed.

As we healed and readied for battle once more, we looked at our loot.

Beyond the enormous polearm with its curved blade, a massive naginata, the wraith-lord also possessed armor that none of us could wear. Perhaps if one of us were a giant?

I noticed that Drek was trying out the naginata. He was strong enough to wield it, but its length, nearly twice his height, made it look comical. It was evident he had experience with polearms, and it was also apparent that he was much better with his axe…

Among the creatures and caskets were gold, silver, and copper pieces, as well as a *Ring of Protection from Evil* and a magical shield. We gave the ring to Clestus and the shield to one of the town guards. I had healed the last of our party, and we lost only one guard in the battle.

"OK, all of that was just to get us here. Now we must face whatever waits… down there," Clestus said aloud, pointing ominously at the stairs.

"Aye, woe be unto them, then!" Drek shouted.

Several cheers from the party.

Smiling, Clestus continued, "Let's descend, Toad, take the lead. The first sign of trouble, fall back."

Toad nodded solemnly, his typical expression. I understood why Clestus had placed him in the lead. Toad was a skilled thief and our best option for detecting a trap before we walked into it.

FLASH

Seeing that a horse could not make it down the narrow steps, I changed back to being a human. I joined the group as we carefully approached the stairs, with Toad taking the lead.

The steps were stone, and as we descended, they reminded me of a castle's turret. Soon, it changed to a straight section of stairs heading down into the blackness beyond our light…

Sure enough, Toad saw something and raised a hand. We all halted. For several minutes, he tapped his dagger on the walls and steps. Something had caught his eye. He quickly stepped to the very edge of the stairway and looked back at us; his unspoken message was clear. We all carefully put our feet on the very edges of the steps.

"Everyone on the edge?" Toad asked.

After everyone said yes, Clestus spoke.

"We are ready, Toad. What did you find?"

Rather than explain, he took out a small but heavy bag. It looked like it was filled with water and was quite heavy. He took out another and held them together. Then, he dropped them on the next step.

SPLINK! SPLISH!

The stairs all snapped into a smooth surface, and from behind us came large rivulets of oil covering the smooth surface.

"Argh! Toad, ye is a master thief, ye!" Drek yelled.

Carefully walking on just the edge, we made our way down the "stairway." It was dark, so I willed sunlight to emanate from me. Clestus cast *Sunlight* as well, so our immediate area was now well-illuminated.

We reached the bottom of the stairs.

The slick, smooth surface of the "stairs" ended in a ten-foot-wide square of open floor with nothing to grab. Again, carefully walking the edge, we worked around the pit and onto solid ground. Looking over the edge, we saw a ten-meter drop to meter-long metal spikes in the gloom below. It would have killed most of the party, for sure.

Clestus whistled.

"Damn, Toad. Thank you," he said, clapping Toad's shoulder.

I swear I saw a hint of a smile on Toad's face.

Taking a look around, I could see the room we were in had no visible doors; it was just a fifteen-meter square room with a three-meter high ceiling. There was a terrible smell in here, one of rot and decay and a whiff of burnt hair.

"What now?" Shivalt asked.

"Hmmm," Clestus was thinking.

Something was amiss, but I couldn't put my finger on it. Finally, I had it. I looked closer at the walls around us—

They were *melting*!

Suddenly, Grey Oozes poured off every wall. They were monsters that looked like stone until they sensed prey. Then, they attacked to cover and dissolve their prey, and they especially liked to eat bones.

"OOZE!" yelled Grace.

We all backed up to the center of the room. The oozes were not intelligent, but their placement here was clever.

As they moved in, there was only one escape—the way we came. Assuming we could get past the pit quickly enough, a slick, smooth incline awaited us. We could never shimmy back up that way in time.

FLASH

I was a unicorn again as missiles and fireballs flew…

I concentrated on one that was near one of our two remaining town guards.

FZZT

In a flash of light, it sizzled and turned to ash.

I saw Drek hit one with his naginata; its amorphous shape shuddered from the strike, and it sizzled. However, it enveloped the weapon and yanked it from his hands. Without so much as a pause, he readied his magical battle axe. It charged him, and he dodged it, hitting it as it went by. His magic axe was clearly hurting it, but it didn't die. One of its gray pseudopods lashed out and grabbed his leg. He screamed as it enveloped his leg and, in one quick movement, flowed all over his body. Struggling blindly, he tried to pull it off.

I couldn't fire without hitting him, so I aimed at another—

FZZT

Another ooze sizzled to ash.

I could see Clestus on the other side of the room. He was using *Body of Flames* and *Fire Jet* again, and quite effectively. The grey oozes realized he was invulnerable to them, as striking him harmed them instead.

I spotted a grey ooze undulating in a pile, where someone was engulfed within its mass. I ran to Drek, who was closer, and began firing less powerful *Sunbolts* at the one that had trapped him. As I shot bolt after bolt, he collapsed and became motionless. Finally, it disengaged to retreat—

FZZT

My full-power bolt turned it to ash.

Turning, I could see the battle was starting to go our way. A town guard had been backed up to the edge of the pit by one of the oozes. His sword was gone from his hand, and he was desperately blocking with his shield. As the ooze latched onto it, he turned and threw it, and the monster, into the pit behind him. Suddenly, a large black pseudopod lunged from the pit and yanked him over the edge.

AHHH!

He vanished from sight, and I heard a nauseating squishing sound; he had been impaled on the spikes in the pit below. Slowly crawling over the edge of the pit, a large blob of darkness emerged.

A Black Pudding.

Even more fearsome than the grey oozes, it lashed out at anything it could find.

FZZT

I fired a *Sunbolt* into it and, in a sizzle and snap, it was now two *more miniature* black puddings.

My *Sunbolt* was doing more harm than good on it, so I turned on the remaining grey oozes. The last town guard had also lost his weapon, probably wrenched from his grasp as well. He blocked the ooze as Shivalt struck it with his magic bastard sword. The ooze fell and lay still.

Turning back to one of the Black Puddings, I noticed that the fire attacks from Clestus and Toad had destroyed the other one.

FLASH

Knowing my *Sunbolts* couldn't hurt it, I changed back to a human again.

Drawing my vorpal sword, I charged it. Sensing me near, it flayed open like a giant wardrobe to envelope me whole; I stopped.

It burst into flames as an *Explosive Fireball*, and a

fire-stone hit it simultaneously, throwing it backward and into the pit.

Squish, Thump.

It must have hit the bottom of the pit but was still alive, and we heard it slithering back up.

"Clestus!" Toad yelled.

I watched as he tossed one of his bags into the pit; he threw in a bag of *fire-stones*!

Clestus ran to the edge and, without looking, fired another *Explosive Fireball* down inside.

KA-BOOM!

Fire and blackness erupted from the pit.

Looking around, I saw the last grey ooze being cut down and lying still. Gulping, I went to the grey ooze that lay dead with a lump inside. Pulling on the form inside, a disembodied, boneless arm came out. Sifting through the monster, we found the boneless form of the town guard. It had dissolved and eaten all of his bones.

I walked over to Drek's motionless body. I could sense life still lingering, but he was dying. He appeared smaller somehow, and I knew some of his bones had probably been dissolved and consumed by the horrible creature.

Thankfully, it was not straining to change forms. Although I had healing spells, nothing was as powerful for healing as unicorn tears. Nuzzling him with my snout, I wept on him.

Standing nearby, I waited. I felt Grace by my side as

she hugged my neck and quietly cried. She was doing exceptionally well. From what I had observed, the other party members were no strangers to combat. However, this was all new to Grace. In just two days, she had witnessed more combat than most would see in a lifetime.

I rubbed against her and licked her arm. She looked up and smiled, and I knew this would be the last time she cried...

Knowing I would be more useful as a human, I stepped away and transformed back once again. As we sifted through the rubble of the pit below, we uncovered quite a bit of treasure.

Nothing mundane would remain, of course, but magic was not easily destroyed by acid.

There was a magic short sword, a *Net of Ensnarement*, and, ironically, a *Ring of Acid Resistance*. Plus, lots of platinum, gold, silver, and copper pieces were scattered about the room. We also found gems, one of which was a *power-stone*.

I knew where it needed to go.

Glancing at Clestus, I tossed it to him. He grabbed it, mulled it over to determine its power, and put it in one of the many pockets on his wizard's robe. He nodded his thanks.

The ring went to Toad, as he was the most likely to need it while dealing with traps and locks. The net went to Shivalt, the most dexterous among us. Finally, the magic sword went to Grace, as she was the only one left who did not yet have a magical weapon. Her attacks against the oozes and pudding were thus worthless, as her now melted sword gave testament.

"Ungh,"

Drek stirred and moaned. Shivalt and Toad assisted him to his feet.

"I dint want to do-er that agin" he muttered.

We all drank water as we rested and then got ready to move out again.

"So, I hate to state the obvious, but… where to from here?" Grace asked.

Toad nodded and started to move around the walls carefully.

Drek and Shivalt followed him while Clestus and I remained prepared to cast spells.

Finally, Toad held up a hand. Then motioned us to step away.

He gently felt a section of the wall. Smiling, he pushed his hand into it, causing a small stone to shift forward. Further down, a ten-foot-square section swung outward, revealing a corridor leading into the darkness.

"Aye, ye be a master thief, fer sure," Drek said.

We ventured deeper into the dungeon…

* * *

THE HALLWAY ahead was sheer stone, like the rest of the dungeon we had been exploring. We moved slowly, with Toad leading the way. I was not alone in my gratitude for Toad. We would never have made it this far without him. Even if we had survived the stair trap, the Black Pudding at the bottom would have made short work of whoever fell in.

I shuddered.

Just because I was accustomed to fighting evil doesn't mean it didn't affect me. I still felt fear, like anyone else.

Toad slowed again; he had spotted something. Despite my keen vision and hearing, I saw nothing, but I was not the professional he was. We all took a few cautious steps back.

We all had faith in Toad, especially now. However, if a trap were sprung, we couldn't help him if we became ensnared as well. We watched Toad take out an empty sack, and then, pulling out a magical waterskin, he poured water into one of the empty sacks. Then, he tossed it far ahead onto a patch of ground. We noticed the floor beneath it dropped a few inches—

SNAP!

A vast expanse of walls, floors, and ceiling was abruptly filled with sharp metal spikes, entirely blocking the hallway. He turned to gaze at us.

"Yipes," Grace said.

We all nodded.

"Thank you again, Toad," Clestus said.

He nodded as Clestus cast *Metal to Mud,* and the spikes plopped onto the ground. We continued forward down the hall. The long hallways contained many more traps, each more intricate and fearsome than the last. All fell to the master thief, however.

The tomb of this mage, Vizerie, was a labyrinth. We were making slow progress, however. We came around a corner and saw a short hallway ending in a stout wooden door. Toad, as usual, took the lead. No more traps were found as we followed him toward the door. As Toad reached the door, we followed a short distance behind.

The ground suddenly shifted!

The floor in front of us dropped twenty feet as the back of the hallway snapped up the same amount. Luckily, we were not too far behind Toad. As we all lost our footing and tumbled, Clestus cast *Wall of Stone*.

We crashed into one another at the bottom in a heap. Looking up, we saw what this trap was. There was an illusion above the ceiling in the back half of the hall. Anyone who had been in the back of the hallway would have gone through the illusionary "ceiling" and been impaled on the spikes above. Those of us past the fulcrum would drop into the end of the hall at high speed. We were all banged up from crashing into each other, but I was sure Clestus's quick thinking saved us all. I didn't even want to know what lay on the other side of that *Wall of Stone* he cast. We all caught a glimpse of blackness beyond the end of our slide; I had no doubt it was a fall into something bad…

Clestus started casting *Stone to Mud* on the ceiling until the back half of the hallway floor was heavy enough to level the floor again.

Toad approached the wooden door. He examined it and then picked the lock.

OWW!

He jumped back, holding his hand. It had a blackish muck on it and was bleeding.

"Damn, lock had a spike come out!" he said.

He poured water on the black muck, causing it to slough off onto the floor, where it *sizzled*.

"Oh, my Lord, that is acid!" said Grace.

We all stared at Toad. The ring on his finger was glowing brightly.

"Wow! Thank you for the *Ring of Acid Resistance*. Guess I would be missing a hand now..." he said.

We pushed open the door and went down another hall; Toad was still in the lead.

This hall was longer and ended in another similar wooden door.

"Stay a little closer this time," Toad said.

We complied, and he retook the lead as we walked down the stone hallway—

AAH!

Toad fell through the floor. There was a loud snap, and we saw blood spray up from below. Three massive, muscular arms came out, each "hand" having three equally massive claws that grabbed Toad and shoved him downward.

Coming out from the ground, like a fish leaping from the water, was a Xorn.

Resembling a giant, bulbous mass of round rock, it had three sides. Each side featured a large, vertically-slit orange eye and a powerful muscular arm ending in three massive talons to grasp prey. The top of its enormous body showcased a gigantic open maw filled with big, sharp teeth. In horror, we watched it snap shut again—

It had swallowed Toad whole.

This creature was not evil, which is why I could not sense it. However, it was ravenous for anything derived from the earth, especially metal and gems… and anyone who might be adorned with them.

It phased out again and slipped below the floor like a shark going back underwater. We separated and watched the floors and walls warily. Turning, I looked at our party.

Without conscious thought, I suddenly grabbed Drek and lifted him off the ground with both hands. Just then, the Xorn emerged beneath us and snapped at where he had been standing. A thrashing sound erupted as Drek, the Xorn, and I tumbled down into a squishy pile of muck.

Moments later, I felt a hand reach in and pull me out; it was Shivalt. Meanwhile, I saw Clestus and Grace pulling Drek out.

I looked down at the quagmire of goo we had fallen into. The entire area under Drek's feet had been turned to flesh with a *Stone to Flesh* spell. The Xorn lay inside it, made entirely of flesh now and quite dead.

With a gulp, I buried my revulsion and reached into its now open maw. Drek helped, and we pulled out Toad's body.

The Xorn had bitten off both of Toad's legs, and there were sharp impalements from its talons all over him. My only hope was that he died quickly and didn't suffocate or bleed to death inside it. We laid him down.

"AGH! Toady, oh my poorest Toady," said Drek with a sniffle.

"Goodbye, good man," Grace said quietly.

There was nothing to be done. So, we took his magical items and coin and moved on.

Reaching the end of a hallway, we saw a stout wooden door. No longer having a thief to check for traps, we erred on the side of caution. Changing into a unicorn, I fired a *Sunbolt*—

FZZT

It blew a hole where the clasp was, and the door swung open. We ventured inside...

CHAPTER 6

As we entered an enormous chamber, we could see a path through the rocky room, with a small stream and a bridge over to the other side. Water dripped everywhere, and it was clear that this was an underground grotto. There, on the other side, was a slight rise to a throne.

Sitting there, staring malevolently with glowing crimson eyes, it watched us.

It was a Lich.

It stood; we could see its tall, gaunt body. Like a skeleton wrapped in flesh, it wore a once-expensive but now tattered imperial cloak. Tiny pinpoints of crimson glowed from its empty eye sockets. In its hands was a jet-black quarterstaff.

Its raspy, unpleasant voice crackled to life—

"I am King Vizerie. One of you has my crown; I can sense it. Welcome, please join me... forever," it said.

It smiled malevolently at us.

FZZT

My *Sunbolt* flew from my horn and shattered the throne behind it while the "lich" merely shimmered.

It was an illusion!

As we closed in on the lich, more undead emerged from the ground and caskets strewn about the room.

Suddenly, I saw Shivalt duck under the mighty swing of Drek's massive naginata. Gracefully tucking into a roll, he emerged in a fighting stance—his sword poised in front of him and ready.

What on Yrth?

That is when I saw it—a tiny, two-hand tall, bright red imp. It was giggling as it "danced," causing Drek to mirror its every move. Luckily, it was not as skilled as Drek; otherwise, Shivalt would be in two pieces now.

FZZT

My *Sunbolt* either partially hit or was close enough to force the imp to dodge, breaking its concentration. Drek lowered his naginata, looking confused.

I saw Shivalt sheath his sword and ready his bow as I fired another *Sunbolt* at the imp.

Its speed, combined with its tiny size, confounded my aim, and I blew a harmless section of the stone wall behind it apart. It giggled at my miss and flew off at high speed.

Twang—THWAK

SQUEAK!

The imp was impaled against the wall. An arrow,

longer than the imp was tall, pinned it to the surface. It hung limply in death.

Shivalt dropped his bow, rolled away from a skeleton's attack, and came up with his sword drawn once more.

My goodness, does he have talent!

Now, my attention shifted to the throng of the undead separating the lich from us. Several were clustered together, charging at me. So, I responded in kind. With my aura of *Protection from Evil* and the sight of a colossal horse galloping at full speed, many scattered in fear.

However, some stood their ground. As I charged in, my sunlight blazing, I lowered my horn. I felt blades strike me from the few who did not scatter. My horn impaled a wight in the chest, and my body obliterated several skeletons as I collided with them at full speed. I slowed to fling the dead wight from my horn. Several more undead were approaching while the rest of the party battled them.

I could see the lich had become emboldened as it cast *Protection from Good* spells onto the undead. It would not save them from our blades, but it made them more challenging to kill.

Continuing my charge once again, I headed for the lich. As I ran over the small bridge, it noticed me and cast a spell. Suddenly, I was no longer moving forward; my feet clawed at empty air.

It had levitated me a whole 10 hands into the air!

I knew that the lich I saw was merely an illusion,

likely a *Permanent Illusion* spell, but it could still cast spells through its eyes. With no way left to harm it, I turned my head and unleashed more *Sunbolts* on the undead approaching me. However, I realized that the real lich must be close to the illusion to control it so effectively.

Frantically, I focused and searched for the source of evil. It was a grueling process due to the overwhelming presence of malevolence in the room. I scanned the walls, moving past the sea of undead. Finally, I discerned its actual location at the back of the room, just behind a wall.

Trusting my intuition, I aimed for the center of what I assumed to be its location—

FZZT

Firing a full blast of *Sunbolt*, I felt awash in fatigue. My *power-stones* could only absorb so much, and they had now run out of energy from the battle. The lich's illusion snapped from existence as I dropped back onto the ground.

I smiled; that would be a successful hit!

Firing repeatedly, I galloped toward that section of the wall, hoping for luck to help me hit it again. Realizing I couldn't make a big enough hole, I turned back to the ongoing battle.

Clestus, as usual, had turned into a creature of flame and was wielding a long stream of fire around him. Several undead lay smoking, with more running about wildly while immolated. More lay on the ground, a victim of Shivalt, Drek, and Grace's blades…

The tide was turning, but the lich was getting away!

WHINNY!

Clestus noticed my distress, turned toward me, and gestured in my direction. The wall hiding the lich transformed into mud and splashed onto the ground. Behind it lay a passage with stairs leading upward.

The stairway was vast, as were the steps, so I took them at a full gallop.

It was risky to run up the stairs at full speed as a unicorn; the steps were wide and made of stone, though. As I galloped up the stairs, I heard footsteps below me. The others had finished the battle and were not far behind. However, with my speed and head start, I would initially be alone against the lich...

* * *

I CAME OUT TO A NIGHTMARE.

Everywhere I looked was aflame. In terror, I realized what the lich had done.

Several Flame Atronachs flitted about, deliberately setting trees and shrubbery ablaze. Luckily, the cold and light snow on the ground conspired against them, but large sections of the forest still burned wildly. There was no tactical reason for it; the lich was simply being malicious and evil.

Concentrating, I reached out with my innate *Beast Summoning* to the animals of the forest—not to call them to me, but to warn them. Any nearby animals should now be fleeing from the deadly forest fire that is developing.

Sensing something dangerously evil, I jumped to my left as a staff whipped through the air where I had been standing.

Vzerie had found me.

It must have cast *Invisibility*, but I sensed something evil at the last moment. Not relenting in its attack, it came for me again. Having no way to parry it, I was forced to run away and create distance before I could counterattack.

As I galloped, I saw several new monsters heading my way now as well. Looking back at the lich, I saw an arrowhead protruding from its left eye.

One of Shivalt's arrows had hit it from behind!

It turned its attention to the rest of the party, who had just arrived.

The rest of the party would be on its own against it without me. In addition to the Flame Atronachs, still quite busy destroying my beloved forest, I saw Direguards.

There were two types of them. First were the Direguard Assassins, tall humanoid figures of abyssal blackness with glowing red eyes set deep within their eye sockets. They resembled wraiths but wielded long, red swords of ethereal malevolence. They phased in and out of our plane as they attacked.

Alongside them were the Direguard Deathbringers. Looking like humanoid demons with curved horns protruding from their skulls, they resembled skeletons clad in plate mail. With glowing green hands and claws, they cut through opponents with green fire and forceful blasts of energy.

It was just them and me now.

As they closed in, I fired *Sunbolts*. Several fell, but the rest reached me. I galloped away as my hindquarters began to shimmy sideways. One of the Deathbringers had hit me with a force blast and claw attack. My hindquarters were numb with pain, but I could still move. Lowering my horn, I impaled an Assassin. It shimmered into oblivion, but not before its ethereal red sword skewered me. Searing pain radiated from my chest, and I could feel blood running freely. Turning back, I saw the last of the Direguards still in pursuit.

I stopped and fired *Sunbolt* after *Sunbolt* at them.

One made it to me and swung its deadly red sword.

Rearing up, I kicked it. Both of my hooves hit its chest, and it flew back and dissolved into the ether. Several of the Deathbringers were still headed my way, dodging my *Sunbolt*s and firing *Cones of Force* at me.

OOF!

Each one struck me like a giant fist.

Finally, it was down to the last one. I shimmied sideways and turned to run. It lunged to catch me before I could get away, its glowing green claws poised to strike my hindquarters.

Unbeknownst to it, I was planning on this. I knew my backside turned to it would cause it to come in for the kill. As I turned, I flexed and then brought up my rear legs and pushed my weight onto my front legs. As it stepped in, my rear legs snapped out, catching it in the chest. I could feel its body snapping as my powerful hooves threw its corpse away from me.

Without a backward glance, I ran for Grace and the fire atronachs. She had left the rest of the party to help me, and they were engaged in mortal combat; she would need my help.

In the distance, with my peripheral vision, I saw the party battling the lich. It cast a *Blink* spell and appeared behind Clestus. Swinging its jet-black quarterstaff, it struck him in the torso.

A mundane staff would have passed through his flaming body harmlessly, but this staff was not mundane...

Clestus's body, now corporeal and no longer one of flames, was knocked sideways, and he fell to the ground in a heap. He was clearly unconscious or dead.

Drek took a hard swing and connected. The lich had a large section torn from its chest, but it was still up. Shivalt also worried it with quick, flashing strikes from his bastard sword.

The skill of the monster was impressive; it really knew how to wield its staff.

Blocking Shivalt, it swiped its staff at his body. Shivalt barely jumped back in time.

As Shivalt and Drek continued their battle, Grace was desperately battling the flame atronachs. Fortunately, she now possessed a magic sword and was defeating them. However, I noticed she had sustained severe burns on several areas of her body, and she was beginning to slow down from her injuries.

FZZT, FZZT

I destroyed the atronachs nearby, and within moments, Grace and I vanquished the last of them.

Acrid smoke filled my nostrils as she leaped onto my back. The forest fire was starting to take hold now, and the blaze was reaching high, lighting up the night sky. Beyond it, the full moon's face laughed down on our plight without mercy.

Without its undead army, still ascending the stairway, the lich was vulnerable. I saw Clestus casting something, and suddenly, the top of the stairway turned to ice. A skeleton about to emerge slipped and fell onto the others; I could hear an avalanche of them crashing into each other as they tumbled down the slick stairs.

The lich lifted its staff, and a blast of black light shot out in all directions.

Suddenly, I could feel evil closing in on us. A *lot* of evil…

If we didn't defeat the lich soon, the undead would overwhelm us. The dungeon we were just in was vast, and the secret exit led to the edge of the forest. However, the graveyard was still nearby. Many more undead were coming…

Shivalt stepped in and attacked the lich in melee. Drek had dropped the naginata and was using his battle-axe against it as well. The lich parried Shivalt's strike and sidestepped Drek's axe attack. Snapping the staff expertly, it struck Drek in the head. Fortunately, between the plate armor and the thickness of the stubborn dwarf's skull, it wouldn't kill him. However, there was another flash of blackness when it struck him, and Drek stiffened like a board, falling over like a fallen tree—he was paralyzed!

Shivalt seized the moment and stepped in, driving his blade deep into the lich.

It made a horrible howling sound and struck his weapon arm with its staff. Releasing his sword, still impaled in the lich, Shivalt somersaulted away. I could see his arm had shriveled, even from here.

As we got close to it, Grace jumped off. She landed and rolled up, drawing her sword again.

The lich now faced us, holding its staff at the ready.

Grace bravely rushed in but was no match for its skill with the quarterstaff. As it struck her with the staff, I witnessed the now-familiar black flash. She was hurled backward and lay still. The creature's weapon clearly bore *Death Touch* infused within it, a magical force that drained life by touching any part of a person.

It turned towards me. I saw Shivalt watching over Grace as the lich, and I slowly circled each other.

With one good crimson "eye" and the other featuring an arrow protruding from where a glowing eye should be, it looked macabre for still being "alive." With Shivalt's sword still lodged in its chest, it was clear that the lich was severely injured.

This was no illusion now.

FZZT

It moved swiftly and nearly dodged my Sunbolt, but I hit it in the arm, which disappeared in a flash of light.

ARGH!

The lich emitted a cry of anguish as its staff fell, useless, to the ground. Without delay, it raised its remaining arm and pointed it at me. Little bolts of light shot from its fingers—*Magic Missiles*. Helplessly, I watched them streak toward me. They exploded on impact, and I shimmied backward as I was struck.

That hurt!

It was time to end this, as it would win a continued ranged combat, so I charged.

The lich cast another spell and was instantly concealed in a pool of darkness. The *Darkness* spell would resist my *Sunlight* and *Sunbolt*, but it was now a battle of wills on whether I would be able to damage it now, or even see it.

It was a close contest, but I won. I could just make out its form in the quagmire of inky blackness. I also felt the immense coldness of another *Fear* spell as I sprinted into it. Lowering my horn, feeling in slow motion even at top speed, I saw it starting to dodge.

Not fast enough, though...

My horn hit it in the abdomen and skewered it through.

As I blasted out the other side of the darkness, all I could see was the lich. It was screaming as it started being engulfed by bright, magical fire.

Slowing to a trot, the last of the lich turned to ash in

the breeze. It joined the rest of the forest cinders as it floated away...

PART IV

EPILOGUE

CHAPTER 7

My priority was healing our party, not just to assist them but also because I needed all of them to help save the forest.

After shedding unicorn tears and casting healing spells on Shivalt, Drek, Grace, and Clestus, I felt exhausted. Shivalt's arm was healing well and appeared normal again, and everyone was either healed or well on their way to recovery. Drek's paralysis eventually wore off, which was fortunate since no one wanted to carry the big lug. Clestus and Grace were simply unconscious and were healed back to normal.

I was exhausted, but there was no time to stop.

Our most effective firefighting efforts, along with the cold weather, the dampness from the recent rain, and the snow covering the ground, ultimately subdued the forest fire. However, it still reduced a large section of my beloved forest to embers and ash.

I cried tears that had nothing to do with healing.

Fortunately, thanks to a natural fear of fire and my warning, most of the animals in the forest survived. Everywhere I looked was blackened by it, and smoke hung heavily in the air.

It had taken us the rest of the night to finish fighting the fire. So, as dawn broke, we returned to town—hungry, weary, and battle-worn.

The townsfolk welcomed us like heroes, and after a well-earned rest, we all gathered at the Lemur for supper, enjoying food and drink.

The banquet was incredible. We enjoyed roasted pig, potatoes, salads, and the lemur's signature bread, cheeses, and meats. The townsfolk had also prepared dishes, creating an abundance of delicious food to savor. With the freely flowing beer, wine, and mead, we all felt stuffed and a little tipsy. Everyone was joyful despite having all experienced loss.

I saw Grace and Shivalt chatting amiably and smiling. I sensed that Grace was still into him, but he seemed a bit oblivious to it. I waited until they finished talking before I spoke to Grace.

"I believe this belongs to you," I said, handing Grace a burlap sack containing the crown.

We had all been sharing my *Bag of Holding*, which could hold numerous items without any weight or mass. I had already handed out the other items in it for the rest of the party.

She smiled and took it, immediately turning to Clestus.

"Mayor," she held out the bag with the crown.

"Thank you. Micah will carefully melt it down in the forge. As agreed, a third goes to you, a third to Darrow's family, and a third to the coffers of the town's defense."

She nodded and put the bag in his hand.

"That is wise; yes, I accept that," she replied.

"All proceeds from found loot will be split among the party members," Clestus said.

"I wish to give all of my coins equally to the families of the slain town guards and the apothecary to help the town," I added.

Clestus looked at me and nodded his head in thanks, then spoke again.

"The council and I have voted in agreement, and we wish to promote Grace to *Lieutenant* Graciela of the village's guard if she chooses to accept," he said, looking at Grace with a smile.

She smiled back at his deliberate use of the third person and responded in kind:

"She does!" Grace said, smiling.

Captain Theodus clapped her back,

"I am thrilled to hear that... *Lieutenant!*" he roared.

We all raised our glasses at her brevetted advancement.

"Aye, too much serious-being fer me, I'll be off in tis afternoon," said Drek.

"Same for me," said Shivalt.

Grace looked shocked and crestfallen at that, but silently came to a decision—

"Excuse me for a moment," Grace said, then grabbed Shivalt and kissed him deeply. We all laughed and cheered. When they came up for air, Shivalt spoke first.

"Perhaps I will stay, just a few more days…"

"Figgered ye might!" laughed Drek.

"Is there anything we can say to change *your* mind, Argent?" Clestus asked.

"No. However, the forest is next to the town… our town, Mayor. I wish also to call this place home, if I may?"

Grace squealed in delight and hugged me as Shivalt put a hand on my shoulder.

"Forever and always, Argent, forever and always," replied Clestus.

We finished our banquet and drinks. Drek was a bit drunk, but the rest of us were still mostly sober. I put on a good face; it was good to feel the warmth of camaraderie, but those we lost weighed on me…

It was late in the day as I walked outside from the pub.

Grace followed me out, as did the others.

"Hooray! Hooray!"

The townsfolk outside had gathered to wish us all well!

We shook hands and hugged until everyone had said their goodbyes. As I turned to walk away, I noticed Drek walking down the road toward the next town and Grace and Shivalt by the pub, now holding hands. Clestus was also watching. Perhaps their village could return to normal again; I certainly hope so.

With a final wave, I turned to my true ancestral home—Hallowdale Forest.

FLASH

I galloped away, my golden hooves and horn glinting in the setting sun's rays...

ACKNOWLEDGMENTS

I wish to thank, first and foremost, my mother.

Without her upbringing and support, I might never have learned to embrace the struggle between Good and Evil, let alone understand the importance of fighting for what is right against what is wrong…

Also, to my beta-readers and editors, my thanks.

I also want to thank an unusual group: role-players. Without the experience of these games in my youth, such as Dungeons & Dragons© and GURPS©, I would have been unable to bring this world to life so vividly.

Lastly, and most importantly, I want to thank you, my reader. Without your support and your enthusiasm, especially about telling others about the books you enjoy, authors would die out…

ABOUT THE AUTHOR

RK Jack is a retired federal agent with over thirty years of experience in federal law enforcement and the military, including many years as an instructor. His background in martial arts, including the use of melee weapons, lends authenticity to his portrayal of adventurers as real people and professional adventurers.

He has always been passionate about teaching and sharing stories, and this book marks his first journey into the thrilling realms of fantasy adventures.

Already an accomplished nonfiction and fiction writer, he mainly writes horror adventures. However, his newfound love of writing has led to more and more creative ideas for his stories…

His journey as a writer has taken a new turn with the exploration of a different genre: dark fantasy.

It turns out that the same terrible monsters that haunt the fantasy world are even more prevalent—and just as horrifying—as those in modern settings.

His debut novella weaves together horror and fantasy—it's not for the faint of heart!

CONNECT WITH THE AUTHOR

I hope you enjoyed this book!

As always, I would greatly appreciate it if you would leave an honest review for this book and/or other books by RK Jack. Your opinion matters a lot!

This is the first book about Argent the Unicorn, with more dark fantasy books to come…

I currently live in Denver, Colorado, and can visit your book club or group upon request. You can reach me anytime through my website: rkjackauthor.com.

Authors everywhere depend on you for them to continue writing their books. So…

Thank you for your support!

Made in the USA
Columbia, SC
28 May 2025